"Damon, what...?"

On his back, done in shades of black, was a large tattoo of a fierce standing grizzly, his front paws extended, claws unsheathed, his teeth bared. Below the bear, it said Running Bear.

"Oh," Thea said. "I...that's your name."

"One of 'em." Her fingers sliding over the words made her realize she had put her hand on his back. "My mother's part Blackfoot. My ancestors fought the system, too—just like me."

"You don't need to fight so hard, you know."

He lifted one naked bronze shoulder. "It's what's inside of me.... And until you think you can handle the inside, you'd better keep your fingers off my outside—if you think you can."

She stuck her hands behind her back, then realized she must look exactly like a little kid ordered not to touch something she could barely resist. Oh, she had seen good-looking men before, but...

One ride on a motorcycle, one taste of freedom, one look at that man's impossibly gorgeous hunky body, and twenty-four years of breeding and reserve crumbled. She was...a sex maniac.

Catherine Leigh lives in a tiny Montana town, surrounded by beautiful mountains and friendly people. The daughter of an American navy admiral, she spent the first twenty-five years of her life traveling the world, but—like her heroines—she fell in love with the Western way of life. Enthusiastically encouraged by her husband and three children, Catherine is now fulfilling her lifelong dream of becoming a writer.

Catherine loves to hear from readers. You can write to her at:

P.O. Box 774
Ennis
MT 59729

Books by Catherine Leigh

HARLEQUIN ROMANCE
3075—PLACE FOR THE HEART
3426—SOMETHING OLD, SOMETHING NEW

Rebel Without
a Bride
Catherine Leigh

Harlequin Books

TORONTO • NEW YORK • LONDON
AMSTERDAM • PARIS • SYDNEY • HAMBURG
STOCKHOLM • ATHENS • TOKYO • MILAN
MADRID • WARSAW • BUDAPEST • AUCKLAND

ISBN 0-373-03469-5

REBEL WITHOUT A BRIDE

First North American Publication 1997.

CHAPTER ONE

THEADORA Birch sank onto the weathered front steps of her great-aunt's ancient Victorian house, folded her arms across her knees and let her sobs come. The letter from Aunt Dora's lawyer dropped from her fingers and began tossing around the untended yard in the breeze.

Thea didn't care. She'd driven all the way from Arlington, Virginia, to Pine Butte, Montana, with a dream in her head—a dream that had been shattered by one walk through Auntie's front parlor. The house had fallen into such disrepair, the task of turning it into the bed-and-breakfast she and Auntie had always talked about seemed overwhelming.

Worse, far worse, Thea couldn't bear the thought that Auntie had lived her last days like this. Why hadn't she told Thea that the big old house had gotten to be too much for her?

She and Auntie had agreed that Thea should finish her two years of apprenticeship as a C.P.A. before she came west. But Thea would have dropped everything and come at once if Auntie had asked. Oh, if only Aunt Dora hadn't been too proud to ask her stuffy old Bostonian family, Thea's family, for a little financial help.

A fresh wave of tears consumed her. Aunt Dora had loved the idea of running a historically accurate B&B as much as Thea had. She must not have asked for help because she hadn't wanted to acknowledge how far the house had deteriorated from the elegant structure Thea remembered.

Since her eleventh summer, the first summer Thea had

spent with Auntie, she'd thought of the old house as the most beautiful place she'd ever lived. And with her father a colonel in the army, she'd lived in plenty all over the world.

Thea's sobs turned to wails. Her father and Chelsea, her half-Cantonese stepmother, would be appalled at such behavior. At the very least, she ought to go inside and wail in private. But she couldn't make herself.

All her life, Thea had lived in big cities where she was rarely out of sight of someone. Auntie's house, nestled in a draw of rolling foothills near the base of Montana's second highest mountain range, gave her a sense of privacy—even on the front porch—she never felt anywhere else.

But it shouldn't, not anymore, not enough to wail outdoors. She'd seen that as she drove up here. New houses abounded. Little groups of small, inexpensive houses, probably lived in by residents of Pine Butte. And big, even ostentatious, houses on large—or vast—lots, no doubt owned by the many wealthy summer dwellers who came here from out of state.

If it wasn't for its eighty-seven acres of sheltering foothills, Auntie's house would be nearly in a neighborhood. True isolation, even in this town of eighteen hundred, was a thing of the past.

At the dim edge of her awareness, Thea heard another sound over her weeping. An easily recognizable sound to a city dweller—the roar of a motorcycle.

The noise grew louder and finally stopped, right in front of her from the sound of it. Overcome by grief, Thea didn't care—she was simply relieved at the sudden silence.

"Who are you?" a rough male voice demanded. "What do you want?"

Thea kept sobbing.

A pause ensued. The man spoke again. "You've got no

business here." Thea didn't respond. "Dammit, what are you crying about?"

Without raising her face, Thea shook her head. She'd explain later. After all, she had every right to be here. Through the blur of tears, she saw a man's booted foot land on the step below her. Black leather, thick sole. As she suspected, the motorcycle person.

She drew a gulping, shuddery breath. "I..." Her throat closed.

"Yes...?" he prompted.

"Maybe she's lost," said a soft female voice.

Thea shook her head again. She rubbed her cheeks against her knees, drying her tears on her slacks, leaving mascara streaks on the beige rayon. It didn't matter; they'd wrinkled so much in the car they already needed to go to the cleaners.

Still she didn't look up. "Do you have a handkerchief?" she asked.

"Yeah, right." Sarcasm dripped from the man's voice. Something unpleasantly familiar about the tone sent a shiver down Thea's spine. "My butler irons a fresh one for me every morning."

She looked around for her purse, remembering she'd left everything except her recipe box in the car. Her quick glance registered a dark man leaning over her, his giant black motorcycle and a beautiful, long-legged brunette sitting on the back of it.

"Well, I'll be goddamned," the man said when Thea raised her face. "Dora said you'd come, but I never believed it."

He regarded her with eyes as dark gray as the ocean in a storm, eyes that disconcerted her, carrying waves of uncomfortable memory. Oh no, it couldn't be! Thea looked quickly away, not wanting to stare long enough to be sure.

"What the hell have you done to your hair?"

Thea ran her hands distractedly over her head. Surely she hadn't been *that* out of control, had she? She knotted her hair too tightly, used too many pins and too much hair spray, for her chignon to come loose no matter how hard she cried. Her hands found a few loose curls—which had, of course, immediately corkscrewed—but no serious disarray.

"The color," he said. "It used to be red, didn't it?"

Oh dear Lord, it was *him.* From beneath her wet lashes, Thea looked again, praying she was wrong. She wasn't.

He hadn't changed much in seven years—but if there had been any softness in him at twenty-one, none remained now. His long hair, blacker than his eyes, needed a cut badly—and a combing after the motorcycle ride that had pulled most of it from his ponytail.

Faded jeans, a black tank top, black boots. He did seem to like the color black. Not surprisingly, the way it made his olive-dark skin and the muscles rippling under it appear. His well-defined shoulders and arms, the sinews of his chest, which the skimpy tank top did little to cover, looked silky dark under the layer of dust he'd acquired riding.

Thea shook off those thoughts and her memories. "My hair color is no concern of yours," she said haughtily, hoping to discourage more personal remarks—more any kind of remarks for that matter. She prayed he'd leave before she had to actually confront him.

He snorted. "I doubt it's the concern of anyone of my sex," he agreed, walking up the steps to examine her from behind. "Color of a mud puddle. You do that on purpose?"

"Oh, c'mon, Damon," said the brunette, climbing off the motorcycle. "Ease up. She hasn't hurt anything."

"Only Dora," he growled.

"What are you talking about?" asked the woman.

Damon put a hand on the back of the woman's neck as she approached. "You wouldn't understand."

Thea wanted to thank the other woman for distracting Damon from her, but her stomach was lurching too violently to speak. Damon Free! She didn't want to remember him, but she couldn't help it. Dora had had enough tact never to mention the man to Thea on the phone, and Thea had certainly never asked about him! But her fond hope that he had left the valley had obviously not come to pass.

With a gulp of determination, she forced herself to stand and pretend that she didn't mind acknowledging him. She should have kept her seat. Even on level ground, he was almost a foot taller than her five foot four. From the step above her, he used his height advantage to tower over her, making her tilt her neck back to meet his eyes.

Memories swamped her. All the fear, panic, distress and guilt…and desire…she'd felt the last time she looked at him on this porch, from just about this angle, hit her again with nauseating force.

For seven years, she had tried to banish the memory, at least rid herself of the disturbing feelings it aroused. But she realized, in one moment of looking into his angry charcoal eyes, all those sensations were in her still, as strong as ever.

Probably strong enough, she recognized, for Damon to read them on her face. Just as he had read her seven years ago…

She hadn't expected to see Damon on that trip. Thea had been on her way from Germany, where Father was stationed, to Mills College in California. Dora had agreed to meet Thea's plane in Bozeman and fly on with her for the rest of the trip, get her settled in at college.

She could hardly wait to get on the plane with Auntie and talk to her heart's content, away from Father and Chelsea's inhibiting presence. It had been so long since they talked in person instead of by phone.

But a thunderstorm grounded their plane overnight.

"Is your car here, Auntie?" Thea asked worriedly, thinking of the long drive to Dora's house.

"Oh, no, child," Dora said. "My eyes are too old for driving at night. But I'm sure the man who drove me to the airport is still here. We'll find him."

As they lifted Thea's many bags from the luggage counter, Dora's friend came up behind them. "I hope you don't need all those for one night," he said. "They'll get soaked in the back of the pickup."

"Oh, Damon," Dora said, "I knew you'd wait. You remember Damon Free, don't you, Thea?"

"Sure she does," Damon said sarcastically. "How could she forget the sinister half-breed juvie she had banished from her presence?"

"Oh, I didn't do that," Thea whispered, blushing and looking around to see if anyone could hear them.

"Could have fooled *me*," Damon said. "One day there I was, visiting my best friend—next day I wasn't even allowed in her house. All because of you."

"I was only eleven, for heaven's sake," Thea protested. "It was Father who—"

"Still blaming the colonel?" Damon flicked up a dark brow. "*You're* the one who told him I'd been busted." He shook his head. "To think I trusted you, Orphan Annie."

"Don't call me that!" she said.

"Children!" Dora said quietly but firmly. "Please behave yourselves."

Damon bent to give Dora a peck on the cheek. "Okay, old lady."

Dora smiled, relieved. "You're a good boy, Damon."

"Yeah, right. That's what everyone says." He chuckled.

The sound shivered down Thea's spine. She remembered that chuckle, the warm way it made her feel, even as a child of eleven, when she got up the nerve to talk to him.

It was the only thing she'd missed about the sullen sixteen-year-old when he stopped coming around. He scared her too much—his anger, his reputation, the insolent look in his dark eyes that seemed to see right through her—for her to dare miss anything else about him.

But it hadn't been her decision to send him away. Of course it *had* frightened her when she learned he'd been arrested for smoking pot, but in a strange way she had also found it rather exciting to have a real criminal visit Auntie every day. In any event, it was Father, not she, who insisted Aunt Dora not allow him in the house, not while Thea was visiting.

At seventeen, Thea felt the very reverse of excitement. How could Auntie look so calm about riding seventy miles in a crashing thunderstorm in a pickup truck driven by a man who might be taking drugs?

But years of daily reminders about manners won out over Thea's fears. The man was Auntie's friend. Reluctantly, she put out a hand to shake.

Ignoring it, Damon gave her a brusque nod and returned his attention to Dora. "I'll find a place to store the extra luggage overnight, then bring the rig to the front." He shot a glance at Thea. "Pick the bags you need." He strode off.

On the long drive to Dora's, Thea grew more and more frightened of the dark, twisting road, illuminated irregularly by cracks of lightning. Sitting stiffly between Auntie and Damon, she tried not to rock into him as the truck swayed around the curves, while she explained to her aunt why she had chosen an all-girls college.

Of course, she couldn't do that without mentioning Father and Chelsea. She felt Damon tense every time she said their names. When she said they'd strongly urged this college because they believed she'd learn more away from the distraction of boys, Damon snorted derisively.

"That old 'Prebble flaw' crap, I bet," he said disgustedly. "Don't tell me they brainwashed you into believing that bull, too."

"Now, Damon." Dora patted Thea's knee. "Damon and I have always talked very openly to each other about our families—their flaws as well as their good points."

Damon snorted. "If we can think of any good points." He lifted one shoulder in a shrug. "Only good thing about Prebbles is they're not quite as stuck-up and narrow-minded as Birches."

Thea bit her lip. "Father always has my best interest at heart."

"You believe *that*," Damon said, "and I've got a bridge in Brooklyn I'd like to sell you."

"Damon, please," Dora said. "Thea is very loyal to her family."

"Stuffy, opinionated bigots," Damon muttered, "don't deserve loyalty."

"Mr. Free," Thea said heatedly, "you don't know anything about my family. They're—"

"I know they're hung up on appearances," interrupted Damon. "Complete bullsh—"

"Damon!" Dora admonished.

He winced, apparently at speaking so in front of Dora. "Sorry, but you sure as hell can't convince me they give a damn about what really matters—what a person's like underneath." He slapped a palm on the steering wheel. "Look what they did to Dora. Banishing her to Montana for getting pregnant with the wrong guy. You can bet they wouldn't have done that if he'd been some third-generation banker or something."

"You know how I feel about that, Damon," Dora said emphatically. "The best thing that ever happened to me was escaping that rigid, structured existence." No one hearing Dora's voice could doubt her sincerity. "I've been very happy here, and you know it."

"That's beside the point. Orphan Annie here knows it, too. That's why she isn't saying anything."

"I, uh…" Thea felt flustered, not knowing how to defend her loved ones. No one ever spoke such things aloud at home. "That was a long time ago. I'm sure they'd react differently today."

"Yeah?"

Damon slammed on the brakes and jerked the wheel hard to avoid a deer leaping across the road. Thea tumbled into Damon, then rapidly righted herself, blushing furiously even in the dark of the car.

Damon simply went on talking as if nothing untoward had happened, but Thea trembled all over, sure every shape she saw at the edge of the roadway was a deer or a moose or a…whole herd of buffalo ready to crush their truck. What if they had to spend the night—or even a few hours— alone here in the dark with this angry man? She tried to concentrate on his words.

"If your old man is so damn liberated in his thinking, why didn't he let you come back and see Dora?" Damon no longer sounded detached; he sounded furious.

Thea felt tears tighten her throat, remembering her misery when Father—still smarting over his wife's desertion the preceding summer—declared *all* Prebbles unfit to help raise his daughter, even for a few months, and refused to let Thea visit Dora again. Thea had tried and tried to convince him, but she'd been helpless against Father's fear that the "Prebble wild streak" would rub off on her.

"Mama—" Thea began, then stopped. She didn't have to explain anything to Damon. Especially these very personal things about her family.

"Right," Damon said. "Exactly my point. Your oversexed mother runs off with some Frenchman half her age, so your old fart of a father won't let you see Dora. That makes a helluva lot of sense.'' He downshifted to take some sharp curves. "You could have stood up for yourself."

"I was only twelve!" Thea cried, gripping the edge of the seat for stability.

"Damon," Dora interrupted, "stop picking on Thea. She was living in Hong Kong, dear boy. She certainly couldn't swim the Pacific."

"Auntie, you know I wanted to come, don't you?"

"Of course I do, child," Dora assured her. "You told me that every time I phoned."

"You could have phoned *her* sometimes," Damon interrupted, slowing the truck to turn off the highway.

Thea grabbed Dora's hand and squeezed. "You understand, don't you, Auntie? Chelsea wouldn't let me. She said—"

"Let's not worry about it anymore," Dora said. "You can telephone me from college whenever you want. Tell them your phone bill's high because you're phoning a rich lawyer's son you met at a cotillion. Say he goes to school back east and doesn't believe in marriage for anyone under thirty." She laughed gaily.

Thea laughed with her. "He'll have blond hair and blue eyes and a weak chin. No lips."

Dora patted her cheek. "If you convince them you like a boy like that, they'll know they've trained the Prebble right out of you."

"Hmmph," Damon snorted. "They blind or what?"

"What do you mean?" Thea asked.

"Can't they—"

"Damon!" Dora said threateningly.

"Never mind, Orphan Annie." He parked the truck in front of Dora's house.

The next morning, Thea came downstairs to have coffee on the front porch, still in her robe and nightgown. Auntie's was the only place she was ever allowed to behave so informally. But instead of Auntie, she found Damon alone on the porch. Embarrassed, she started back inside, but his taunting voice stopped her.

"What are you so afraid of?" he asked. "What do you think will happen to you out here?"

"I'm not afraid." Thea turned around. "I'm just improperly dressed for outside...with a strange man."

"I'm not that strange."

"You know what I mean. I don't know you." She was trembling...no doubt from embarrassment. She wondered nervously where on earth Auntie was and why Dora liked this odious man.

But she was determined not to let him see he scared her. And what was she really afraid of anyway? He wouldn't hurt her. He was Auntie's friend—heaven knew why.

"I'm not scared," she repeated, trying to sound less timid.

Damon rose and came toward her. "Hell you're not."

"I...you..." He stood so close she couldn't think.

"I'll prove it," Damon breathed.

He lightly took her arms, running his palms softly from her shoulders to her elbows. Though Thea would have said no space remained between them, Damon stepped closer. When Thea backed away, Damon chuckled. The warm sound made her soften toward him even though she knew she should be pulling her arms free and running from him.

If she asked, he'd let her go; she could tell. He didn't hold her with a vise or anything. He only held her with... She couldn't explain it. Chewing her lip, she took another step back and bumped into the wall of the house.

Damon came up against her. "Still want to know what your blind parents can't see?" he asked. "Want to know where their plan failed? Cotillions and girls' colleges aren't enough, are they?"

"What *are* you talking about?" Thea said, then shook

her head. "Never mind, I don't care to know what you think."

"That's 'cause you already know," Damon said, chuckling. "Same thing you're scared of now. And it ain't me."

"I'm not scared of anything." Thea's voice was infuriatingly wobbly.

"Scared your stuffy old man all to hell. But his edicts didn't do the trick, did they?" Damon chuckled again and dipped his head toward hers. "I could tell last night, the way you quivered every time you touched me."

She felt his warm breath on her cheek that made her quiver, too. "I didn't. I was simply afraid of the thunder."

"Ri-ight," he murmured, his lips brushing hers. "You got it, Prebble, just like your mama. Maybe like your aunt. And you want *this*, just like me."

His mouth covered hers, and Thea closed her eyes in...anguish. Dear heaven, they were outside! Anyone could see them. Dora might catch them. Worst...or best, as his lips softly massaged hers open, Thea knew his kiss would not be like any other she'd ever received. This was no boy she kissed now; everything about him was full grown and all man.

Swept away, overwhelmed, Thea realized her mouth was opening to his pressure, letting his tantalizingly rough tongue slip inside her. The intimate feel of sharing her mouth with a man shocked her.

She made a startled noise and shoved against his shoulders, trying to push him away. But he swallowed the noise, and her hands on his shoulders didn't budge him an iota. He pressed his long male body against her tender inexperienced one.

With nothing between them but light cotton and rough denim, Thea couldn't help feeling his hardening desire. It

touched her in a way she found frightening .... disturbing...
and utterly delicious. Her struggles ceased— or rather they
changed character.

Something inside her seemed to open up in response to
Damon, to soften, to welcome the profound maleness of
him. A longing flashed through her, melting her belly, turning it to a quivering fire of desire. Frantic at the new sensations, Thea struggled to get closer to him. Her hands fluttered helplessly over his chest, behind his neck, down to
his waist. Her startled sound changed to a moan of longing
and she clutched him tighter.

Damon's chest heaved with raspy breaths and he lifted
his head, disengaging from their kiss. He still held her arms
as if she would drop if he let her go. Thea's head tipped
back against the wall of the house and she closed her eyes
in despair.

"See what I mean, Prebble?" Damon whispered.
"You've got it good."

"No, I don't. This isn't the way I am." Thea didn't think
she was making sense, but she had to fight him somehow.
At least she had to convince herself that none of this was
really happening. "I don't...feel this way."

"You can't fight it, Prebble—you probably had it in the
womb."

"No!" She shrugged free of his grasp and ran into the
house...

For seven years, Thea had fought the memory, believing
she had ultimately lessened its impact on her. But as she
gazed at this lean, dark man she'd prayed never to see
again, the memory rose with all its old intensity, making
her squirm in humiliation.

Here on the very same porch, with Damon Free looking
down at her, his dark eyes letting her know he remembered
the kiss as well as she did, she couldn't deny any of it.
Worse, she knew with certainty that he also remembered

her response to him, would be glad to describe it in mortifying detail if she did anything so foolish as to pretend it had never happened.

He confirmed that with his next words. "That when you dyed your hair, Prebble?"

Too shaken to tell him that was none of his business, Thea blushed furiously. But she'd be darned if she'd admit to this arrogant male that she'd done so the very next week.

Looking at her flaming cheeks, Damon chuckled.

The sound had its usual trembly effect on Thea. She stiffened her spine in resistance and backed off the step. Looking around the yard, she saw the letter blown against the trunk of a tall pine tree and went to retrieve it.

When she turned, Damon was listening to his rider as she held one of his hands in both of hers and spoke heatedly but quietly to him. He shook his head angrily and walked away from her to the end of the porch. Grabbing the railing, he stared out over the lake toward the mountains. The sun lowering behind the peaks, glaring into his eyes, didn't seem to bother him.

Thea caught herself gazing at his muscular back and thighs and...buttocks. Blushing, she cleared her throat and held up the letter. "Auntie's lawyer, a Mr.—"

"Silas Thorton."

"He sent me a key to the house and said I could stay here." She looked at the letter again, as an excuse not to meet Damon's assessing eyes. "So you see I have more right to be here than you."

"More?" Damon walked slowly toward her, his boots making a heavy sound on the weathered boards of the porch. "You're assuming a lot, aren't you? The letter *I* got said the will reading wouldn't take place till tomorrow."

"Well, um, yes...that's right. I just..." Heat stole into her cheeks. "Auntie always said..."

"Yeah?" Damon continued to regard her like something

stuck to the sole of his shoe. He stood close enough now for her to smell the dust on his jeans, a faint odor of male sweat. "How do you know what she promised me? For all you know, we might be having a big sale here in a week or two."

"Sale?" Thea protested. "You'd sell Auntie's house or precious antiques...just for money?"

"*Just* money?" Damon retorted. "What the hell else would I sell them for?" He strode to his bike and straddled it. "Have you seen the house? Forget living there. No one from your family could stand it. Sell the land and get your tail back to Boston."

"I live in Virginia now," Thea said, clenching her fists. "And you know nothing about my family, no matter what you think."

Damon shrugged. "More than I want to know, believe me."

He pushed the machine off its kickstand and the brunette climbed onto the seat behind him. Thea suddenly realized how dreadfully rude she'd been to this woman.

"Aren't you going to introduce me to your wife?" she asked.

"Why bother?" Damon said. "You won't be here long enough to get to know her." He looked over his shoulder at the woman as she slid her arms around his waist. "Right, babe?"

She shook her head. "You're being awful, Damon." She turned to Thea. "I'm not his wife, honey. Who would be crazy enough to marry him?"

Laughing, Damon kicked a pedal on his motorcycle and it jumped forward. Seconds later, he and his woman were hidden by the rapidly receding dust cloud whipped up around them.

CHAPTER TWO

REMEMBERING the groceries she'd bought, Thea retrieved them from the car, but hesitated with her hand on the handle of the screen door. Directly ahead of her was the overwhelming task of restoring Dora's house to its deserved former grandeur. Damon's words had made the job seem even more daunting.

The outside was bad enough. It badly needed paint, probably a new roof, a rain gutter and several railings, and one of the chimneys had lost some bricks. But inside, with some rooms closed off, the furniture draped with sheets and plastic of all descriptions, some windows boarded...

Swallowing her anxiety, Thea entered the house, though not with complete calm. Auntie had never cared a lot about cooking, so heaven only knew what state she'd let the kitchen get into.

As Thea put the sack on the counter and looked around, her knees actually trembled with relief. The kitchen looked clean and well cared for. Auntie must have devoted her efforts the past few years to the rooms she used regularly.

The big oak table, an antique Auntie had restored years ago, gleamed. Copper tiles, tarnished but clean, covered the counters and backsplash. The glass fronts of the built-in cupboards, if they didn't quite sparkle, at least were clean of fingerprints. And the cherry wood glowed naturally.

Auntie had painted over much of the woodwork in the rest of the house; thank heavens she had skipped the kitchen. Thea vaguely remembered a phone call years ago when Auntie told her fresh paint drove out mice...or was it spiders? She hadn't paid much attention at the time. It had never occurred to her that Auntie would paint over the beautiful wainscoting in the house they both loved.

Thea hoped the kitchen's pristine condition meant that the other rooms Auntie used—her den, her bedroom and her workshop—would look as good. But she decided she wouldn't look in the workshop, Auntie's very favorite place, till daylight.

She began to put away the groceries. For that matter, she wouldn't take a serious tour of the three upstairs floors in the dark, either. The attic had always been home to a few mice; by now they'd probably migrated to lower floors. And she didn't think she could bear to look in Auntie's bedroom all by herself.

Especially since she had yet to make her promised call to Father. As Thea took out a couple of eggs and a green pepper for an omelette, she admitted to herself that she didn't want to tell Father all the details about the condition of the house. She knew how discouraging he could be. This way, she could tell him truthfully she hadn't yet had a chance to really see the place.

Her shoulders slumping in resignation, she put down the skillet she'd dug out of the cupboard and turned to the phone. The bell at the other end rang less than once.

"Colonel Birch," Norman answered.

"Father, it's Thea. I made it."

"You missed your ETA by a considerable margin, didn't you?" he said. "It must be almost twenty-one hundred hours out there."

Thea decided not to disabuse him of his erroneous notion that she had just arrived. "I hope I didn't wake you."

"No indeed, Theadora. I told you I'd wait for your call. Chelsea went to bed some time ago, but asked me to wake her when I heard from you." Norman sounded brisk, as if impatient with this chitchat. "How does the house look?

No vandalism, I hope. That often happens to deserted houses.''

"Not here, Father," Thea said. "The lawyer told me he'd hired a caretaker.'"

"Now that you've seen it, how much do you think the old place is worth?" Norman asked.

Thea gritted her teeth. "I have no idea. I told you, I just got—''

"Yes, yes," Norman interrupted. "But you must have an idea what condition it's in."

"It'll need a lot of work even to get it ready to sell," Thea told him. "It's nearly dark now and I haven't looked it over thoroughly. But I'd say it needs extensive renovation.''

"Unfortunate." Norman didn't sound a bit sympathetic. "Best to simply raze it and sell the land then."

"Raze it?" Thea choked. "Auntie Dora's house? *My* house? Father, I love this—''

"Now, Theadora," Norman cut her off. "You're not getting any crazy sentimental ideas again, are you? I *knew* I shouldn't have let you talk me out of accompanying you on this trip. Don't tell me you're starting that hotel nonsense again." He made a disgusted noise. "My daughter— an innkeeper! Pfaugh! Shall I fly out to help you make the decision?"

Much as she wanted to, Thea didn't really consider hanging up on him. He'd catch the next plane. "No, Father, of course not," she assured him, as an image of Damon in motorcycle leathers greeting Father in dress uniform brought a grin to her lips. "But I can't make a proper assessment of the house's value in a few minutes. It's a historical structure, remember. It's possible that a reasonable investment in restoring the house could pay off. The housing market seems to be booming out here.''

Thea felt sick talking about Dora's home this way, as if

it meant nothing more to her than a deposit to her bank account. But she couldn't let Father fly out here. She'd never be able to stand up to his pressure, especially if he brought Chelsea.

"Very well," Norman said grudgingly. "But I expect you to use the same hardheaded approach you use for your clients. Remember the operative word here is *reasonable* investment—in terms of money, time and your efforts. Don't put too much heart in it, Theadora. You know how attached you get."

"You're right, Father." Thea would agree with anything now just to get him off the phone.

She hadn't lied to Father since she was three years old. She was trying very hard not to now—not directly. But she knew she was dancing around the edges of the truth, trying to mislead him. That made her very uncomfortable and had every time they'd discussed Auntie's old house.

On top of all the other problems she would face turning this ramshackle old dwelling into a B&B, she couldn't handle fighting Father every step of the way. If she could just get the renovation really under way before he knew her plans and flew out here to discourage her, she'd have a better chance of going ahead in the face of his opposition.

If she had to be a little evasive on the phone to hang on to her dream, she would. But she hated it.

"The will reading is tomorrow?"

"Yes, Father."

"Call me afterward—when we really know where we stand."

We? Thea wanted to cry. *Did* you *get a letter from Dora's lawyer?*

"Yes, Father."

"I'll tell J.P. you sent your best," Norman said peremptorily. He hung up—as always—without saying goodbye.

My best! The only thing I'd like to send that jerk is a

black eye, Thea grumbled to herself as she finished making her omelette.

Of all the men Father had ever selected for her, J. P. Crawford was the absolute worst—and Father's absolute favorite. Or was his family's brokerage firm Father's favorite? No matter, the two were inseparable.

J.P. hadn't started a conversation in which he, or his money, was not the principal topic of discussion since she'd met him. Worse, his touch made her skin crawl. Not that good ol' J.P. had noticed. She had to fight the creepy octopus off after every date.

Why, even that awful Damon Free couldn't hold a candle to J. P. Crawford when it came to… Thea couldn't think of a term bad enough to express her distaste.

But maybe Father and J.P. had done her a favor.

Would she really have found the nerve and initiative to make this trip, defy Father, quit her job, put all her hopes in one shaky dream, if she didn't have J. P. Crawford hanging over her head? Independence had become ten times more attractive since she realized that Father actually wanted her to marry that self-satisfied oaf.

After dinner, Thea flicked on the hall lights that should have illuminated the wide, elegant stairway to the second-floor landing. But burned-out bulbs in most of the ancient fixtures left the upper part of the stairs in darkness.

When she peeked in Dora's den and found it habitable, she decided to sleep on the old leather couch. Another bulb burned out with a flicker. Thea gave up all thought of upstairs and brushed her teeth at the kitchen sink. By the time she crawled into her sleeping bag, she felt so sleepy and drained she was sure the lumps in the old couch wouldn't trouble her at all.

In minutes, she was asleep. Minutes later, she was awake. The old house made so many unfamiliar noises, Thea spent hours being torn from sleep by creaks and groans that for some reason reminded her of the roar Damon's motorcycle had made coming down the road. At midnight, the chiming of the grandfather clock Auntie had restored and built into a corner of the entry hall woke her completely.

In desperation, Thea flicked on the den light and got the *Journal of Accountancy* from her briefcase. Her eyelids finally fluttered heavily shut—just as a pinky lightness grew over the mountains to the east.

Thea woke to pounding. With a jolt, she jumped up and stood, dazed and confused, in the brightly lit den. A fresh spate of knocks on the front door brought her fully awake. She looked around. Sunshine poured through the windows.

Grabbing her robe and pulling it tightly around her, Thea walked cautiously to the front door. "Who is it?"

"Well, who the hell do you think?" Damon's voice had no trouble penetrating the thick wooden door. "No one else knows you're here. Except Silas Thorton, and he sent me up here to find out what's the matter with you." He rattled the knob. "Want to open the damn door? Dora never locked it in seventy years."

Thea tightened her sash and opened the door. "I'm sorry. I overslept. I didn't get to sleep till…I'm not sure, but the sun was coming up."

Damon raised a brow. "I saw lights on in the den this morning," he said. "I thought that meant you were up, not sleeping in."

"Saw my lights?" Thea held the neck of her robe with one hand. "What were you doing—peeking through the drapes?"

"Hell no," Damon snorted. He gestured toward the east. "I work construction at a house down on the lake. Saw your lights from the road when I went to work."

He works? Thea pushed her fingers through her hair,

grimacing at the feel of her out-of-control curls. "I must have been just going to sleep."

Damon cocked his head at her. "What kept you up? Dora haunting the old place?"

"Don't be ridiculous, Damon," Thea said. "I'm just not used to the noises of an old house." She had no intention of telling Damon that she'd thought more of his deafening motorcycle and their disturbing conversation.

He looked impatient. "Fine. I'll wait for you and give you a ride to Silas's office for the reading." He ran his dark gaze over her tousled, undressed form. "How long will it take you to get ready?"

"A ride?" she asked, swallowing nervously. "On your *motorcycle*?"

His chuckle reminded Thea to keep up her guard around this untrustworthy man. "I've got my pickup. *I* was at work, remember, not sleeping the morning away."

"I can drive my—"

"Sure you can, but it'll be faster if I do it. I know where we're going." He aimed a thumb at the upstairs, obviously assuming that's where she'd slept. "Get dressed and I'll call Silas and tell him we're on our way. More or less."

Thea pursed her lips. "I haven't even had coffee."

"I've got a thermos in my truck." He sounded more impatient with each word. "Just get going, will you? I want to get this over with."

Thea turned, skirted the wide stairway and continued to the back of the entry hall.

"The bathroom's upstairs."

"I need to get my things."

She didn't turn to face him, just stepped quickly into the den. But a moment later when she emerged with her cosmetics and toiletries, she nearly ran into his large body, which he had planted right outside the den door. He stood with his legs braced apart, his hands on his hips.

"You slept in the den?" He didn't smile, but his charcoal eyes held a spark of humor.

"Yes, I did," she said primly. "I couldn't bear the thought of sleeping in Auntie's bed and it was too late to—"

"Right," Damon interrupted, laughing now. "Afraid to go to her room in the dark, weren't you? You really do believe in ghosts."

"No, Damon, I—"

He stood aside. "Well, get going. I'm sure she won't join you in the shower. I don't think she needs showers anymore, do you?"

"Mr. Free," Thea said, holding her head high, "you are the most insolent thing I have ever met. I would appreciate it very much if you will wait *outside* while I dress. It's completely inappropriate for you—"

"If you step on it," he said. "I'll give you ten minutes."

"Ten minutes?" she squawked. "It'll take me at least forty-five."

Damon groaned. "I was afraid you'd say something like that." He rubbed the back of his neck. "I'll be back in an hour."

Breath she hadn't realized she was holding gushed from Thea's lungs as the door finally shut behind Damon's broad back. That man was the most unsettling human being she'd ever met. She couldn't understand why Dora had been so fond of him. Of course, Damon probably didn't bully Dora this way, but even so...

Just looking at the man made her nervous. It was more than her uncomfortable memories of him. With his dark eyes, his deep voice and black hair...he had too many muscles and too few manners and...he was *exactly* the kind of man her mother always seemed to marry. After she left Norman, that is.

And when Thea made the mistake of standing near

Damon, she felt as if she'd gotten too close to a powerful, barely restrained force. Perhaps it was his resentment; he made no effort to hide his lingering hostility over his…"banishment" years ago. And he *certainly* showed no respect for the proper professional demeanor Thea had spent years cultivating.

Every time Damon left, she felt as if she'd survived something…a storm, a battle. Perhaps that had kept Auntie young, all that energy. It exhausted Thea. Thank heavens he'd had the perception to leave her alone for an hour, instead of pacing her entry hall while she bathed in the nude.

Well, of course in the nude, she thought, turning on the hot water. How on earth else would she bathe? But thinking of that dark-haired man pacing downstairs, or even sitting outside in his truck, made her intensely aware that she had nothing on as she hung her robe and nightie on the hook on the back of the bathroom door.

When she returned to the den to dress, Thea was appalled to hear the grandfather clock chiming noon. Dora had set the clock to chime only at twelve—noon or midnight— which was often enough, she said, to know the time. Thea had slept in nearly till noon! She hadn't slept past eight o'clock since she was a teenager. Father and Chelsea would cringe. For that matter, Thea cringed. She—

Damon didn't knock this time. He simply opened the front door and shouted, "You ready? Silas expects us in fifteen minutes."

Swallowing her irritation at his presumptuous entrance, Thea emerged from the den. "Really, Damon," she said, "it would make more sense for me to drive myself. I can follow you. Then you won't have to bring me all the way back out here."

"Not a problem," he said, but Thea noticed a slight tightening of his jaw.

"Damon, I'm perfectly—"

He made a cutting gesture with his palm. "Listen, Prebble. I promised your aunt I'd do this. You can stand here and argue with me all you want, but when you get down to Silas's office and realize what you're listening to, it's going to make you damn sad."

Thea let out a shaky breath. "I'm sure you're right."

"Exactly." He opened the door and waited for her to exit. "Dora knew that. She...suggested that I put aside my resentments for a few hours to do her this last favor. And I will."

Thea turned at the bottom of the steps. "I am not a...simply a...favor for Auntie. I can—"

Damon put his palm in the small of her back and propelled her toward his pickup. "Just get in the truck."

Thea hurried forward, eager to put distance between her body and the disturbing touch of his large warm palm. Large, warm, *male* palm. She jerked open the truck door and climbed inside, berating herself for such nonsensical whimsy. How on earth could she tell his palm was male simply by the touch? She might as well believe in ghosts.

She squirmed against the seat back where the sun had heated the dark plaid upholstery. Except, she noted, Damon had parked his truck in the shade.

But she couldn't let herself believe the comfortable warmth spreading up her spine was the lingering effect of Damon's hand on her back. Just because she could still feel the imprint of each finger didn't mean...

Damon climbed in the driver's side. "Better buckle up," he said. "We're late."

Silas Thorton's office reminded Thea of a gaslight-era play, a high-school play. Dora had restored a turn-of-the-century desk for Silas several years ago, Damon told her during their too-fast drive to town, and the lawyer had redecorated his whole office to match. But the other pieces looked phony and out-of-place next to Dora's work.

Silas, in a light cotton suit, didn't seem to go with the desk, either. "So sorry about your aunt," he said, gripping Thea's hand. "I know how much she meant to you."

Damon muttered something and dropped into one of the armchairs in front of Silas's desk. Silas shot him an irritated glance as he gestured Thea into the other chair.

He picked up a legal-size document backed in blue paper. "I'm going to read all of Dora's will to you, word for word, but I want to explain something to you first."

Thea traced her finger over the tufted leather on the arm of her chair. Damon was right. Hearing this would make her sad, and she wished Silas would just read the cold legal words and get it over with.

"I'm sure I'll understand it, Mr. Thorton."

He slipped on a pair of wire-rimmed reading glasses. "I'm sure you would, too. But I'd prefer to do it this way. Dora wrote this will several years ago, when she was in somewhat better circumstances."

Thea chewed hard at her bottom lip, trying not to cry. "Why didn't she let me know? I'd have come at once. Our family would have helped if—"

Damon growled an oath, his tone clearly disbelieving.

"They would!" she insisted.

Silas held up a palm. "I know that. Dora knew it, too, but she didn't want to ask them." He paused and cleared his throat. "I've been managing Dora's money for a long time. That is…I've sort of watched while she managed it herself."

Damon grunted affirmatively. "Dora didn't take too well to people bossing her."

Thea nodded wistfully, wondering as she so often had before where Auntie had gotten her amazing strength of character. It wasn't the sort of trait Mama's family revered in its women.

Silas continued. "In the past few years, she had some...setbacks."

Thea looked up sharply. "I'm a C.P.A., Mr. Thorton. You don't need to speak to me—" she shot a glance at Damon, who looked as if his face was carved of granite "—to us as if we're idiots about financial matters."

"Right," he said. "Five years ago, about the time she wrote this will, Dora gave a large chunk of money—a hundred thousand dollars to be exact—to an organization that funded women's shelters and promised them another hundred thousand when she died. A year later, she gave them a hundred and fifty thousand more."

"Why, that's a quarter of a million dollars," Thea said, "even before the bequest."

"Yes," Silas said. "But at the time she wrote the will, she was worth about a million dollars."

"A million dollars!" Thea exclaimed. "Then why didn't she keep up the house?"

"The house and the land are a large part of her net worth," Silas explained. "Especially the land, the way everything's developing up there. Dora's sheltering hillsides and lakefront footage...well, the value goes up every year. But, of course, land's not liquid. After her last gift to the shelter, she slowed down on her antique sales. At the same time, a few of her investments decreased in value."

"I understand liquidity, Mr. Thorton." Thea glanced at Damon, who had barely moved a muscle since this discussion began, then back at Silas. "Surely you don't think I'm worried about the size of my inheritance?"

"Perhaps not, but to leave another hundred thousand dollars to the women's shelters, Ms. Birch, will take most of the liquid assets of the residuary estate." He looked at her over his glasses. "It was something Dora cared about very much, single women with young children and no place to go."

"I know," Thea said. "She never forgot how she felt when she was young and alone with a baby. Even after her daughter died, she..." She tried again to swallow the lump in her throat.

"When I explained to her last year that her estate had changed, Dora didn't bother with a new will," Silas went on. "Instead, she wrote a codicil, making three changes. First, she appointed you, Damon, as executor of her estate."

"Ummph," Damon grunted.

He'd been so quiet she would have forgotten someone else was in that chair. But even silent, Damon exuded an energy that kept Thea from being entirely comfortable.

"It surprised me," Silas said, "but I couldn't talk her out of it. Second, she made the bequest to the women's shelters conditional on your approval, Ms. Birch. If you prefer to spend the money on the house..."

"Oh, I wouldn't dream of taking money from the shelters," Thea said.

"Very well," Silas said. "As long as you understand, I'll read the will."

He began reading in a dry tone that should have disguised his personal feelings for Dora, but didn't quite. Dora made a small bequest to the Pine Butte Public Library, a special bequest to her dear friend, Damon Running Bear Free, and the rest of her estate to her beloved niece and namesake, Theadora Prebble Birch.

Dora had written a letter to Damon, which she asked Silas to read before he revealed the amount of the bequest, which had also been changed in the codicil. From the corner of her eye, Thea could see Damon's fingers turn white around the arm of his chair. Other than that, he made no movement.

"Darling Damon," read Silas. *"Please understand that this money is for you. You may spend it on beer and motorcycles, a vacation, women, invest it, give it away. Whatever moves you, pet.*

"You will realize at once, of course, what I wish you would spend it on, but I am not such a senile old lady that I expect that. It's just a dream, and I know it.

"I understand what I would be asking of you if I asked it, so please believe, Damon, I am not asking. Unless you see—as I do—the good of it for you, do not even consider it. Your friendship has meant more to me than I can say, Damon. Thank you for everything, including bringing Thea here today, which I'm sure you did for me. All my love, Theadora Prebble."

Thea thought either Damon's fingers or the chair arm would break any second. Suddenly, he shot to his feet and shouted, "No!" He stalked toward the door as if he meant to leave, then turned to face them. "No, goddammit, no!" He shook a fist at Silas. "Don't tell me. Damn her! That devious, sneaky, underhanded old woman!"

Stunned, Thea stared, her jaw dropping nearly to her chest. What was Damon shouting about?

Silas was less startled. "Don't you want to know how much—"

"I know how much. She's leaving me $154,776, isn't she?"

"And eighty-four cents," Silas said, nodding.

"No!" Damon yelled again.

"No?" Thea asked weakly. Could this be the same man who last night had threatened to sell off Dora's antiques for the money?

Thea had a strong feeling Silas and Damon understood something she didn't. She opened her mouth to ask, but Silas waved her to silence.

"Dora was awfully good to you, Damon."

"She was a helluva lot more than that to me, Thorton, and you know it!" His voice had risen with every word, and he was now shouting at the top of his lungs. "But I still won't do it. Damned back-stabbing old...sneak!"

Silas looked exceedingly disapproving. "It's the last thing she'll ever ask of you, Damon, and she never asked you for much. My understanding is that most of the giving went the other way."

"Don't try that guilt trip on me, old man," Damon growled. "It won't work." He made a visible effort to control himself. "Can't I just refuse it?"

Refuse one hundred and fifty thousand dollars? Thea's eyes felt like they were popping out of her head as she stared at Damon.

"Yes," Silas said. "Then it would return to the residuary estate and be part of Ms. Birch's inheritance." He stabbed a finger at Damon. "But Dora—for some reason, perhaps senility—wanted you to have it."

"Hell she did," he said. "No way would she want me to take it and fritter it away. Or even stick it in a savings account and blow the interest. You know damn well what she wanted done with it, and there's no way in hell I'm going to do it." Damon pulled open the door. "Only chance that money has of being put to the use Dora wanted is if I refuse it. And I do!"

Silas drew back in his chair and steepled his fingers together. "I profoundly hope Dora can't hear you now."

Thea looked from one man to the other, wishing just as profoundly that she understood anything about this conversation.

"Oh, no, you don't, Silas," Damon growled, his frown deep and furious. Then his expression crumpled and he drew a hand down his face. "If Dora can hear us," he said, his voice quiet now, "she understands. It's better for Thea to get it than me. She's more…respectable. She'll do what Dora wants.''

"Of *course* I will," Thea interjected. "Whatever Dora wants…wanted. But surely—''

"You know perfectly well she can't," Silas said acidly to Damon, as though Thea hadn't said a word.

Damon just glared at him.

Thea's thoughts swirled with confusion. What could Damon handle that she couldn't? And, after everything he'd said about his friendship with Dora, what could Auntie ask that he'd refuse to do—so adamantly? She wished one of these men would quit arguing and explain, preferably Silas, who could likely do so with less strain on Thea's hard-won composure.

Silas looked dismayed, but he quit debating the point. "Will you accept the appointment as Dora's executor?"

A barrage of emotions crossed Damon's face, primarily unrelieved grief. "Yes, dammit, all right, I'll do that much."

He left the office, closing the door loudly, just short of a slam.

CHAPTER THREE

STUNNED, Thea stared a moment at the door Damon had all but slammed, then turned back to Silas. She must have looked confused; she certainly felt it.

"Well." Silas exhaled gustily as if he'd been holding his breath. "That went about as I expected."

"It did?" Thea asked, annoyed. If Silas had known how much the bequest would shock Damon, why hadn't he made some effort to give him the news more gently? He'd certainly treated Thea with that kind of courtesy.

The lawyer simply shrugged. "I warned Dora. I was quite sure that young man wouldn't live up to her expectations, and I told her so. But she insisted she knew him better than I do."

"What's this all about?" Thea asked. "What made him so angry? Why would he refuse the money if Dora wanted him to have it? She must have been very fond of him to leave him such a gift."

"Indeed she was." Silas fiddled with a paper clip from his desk. "Damon Free has been pulling the wool over Dora's eyes since he was thirteen. He was very careful not to reveal to her his, uh, baser nature."

"How can you talk that way?" Thea asked. "Auntie helped lots of unhappy kids. She was seldom fooled."

"No one's a hundred percent." Silas refolded the will and tucked it into a manila folder. "I think perhaps that's all I should say. Small town, you know. You'll learn quickly enough all you need to know—probably more than you want. Suffice it to say the rest of us see a very different side of Damon's character than your aunt did."

36

Thea tapped a fingernail against the leather arm of the chair. "How can I learn anything in this town," she asked, "if everyone keeps walking off—" she gestured at Damon's empty chair "—or refusing to speak? After all, Silas, I *am* Auntie's heir. I need information to make decisions about the house."

"Well, as to that," he said, "perhaps you should call the lumberyard. Speak to Marsha, the owner. She can help you with that sort of decision. But, um..." Silas paused, long enough that Thea thought he wasn't going to finish this thought, either. "You'd better take everything she says about Damon with, er, a large lump of salt. They were close, *very* close, for a while—if you take my meaning. May still be for all I know." He pursed his lips in disapproval. "If she speaks highly of him, you'd better ask yourself just what it is she thinks he does so well."

Thea was blushing hotly by the end of Silas's speech. But he seemed to expect a response. "I might have seen her yesterday. When Damon came by the house, he had a woman on the back of his motorcycle."

"Caretaker!" Silas slapped a palm on his desk. "I warned Dora about that, as well, but she wouldn't listen. Insisted Damon could handle it. That's his idea of watching the house—to ride that infernal machine by the house with one or another of his chicky babes clinging to him. Did this woman have short, frizzy hair always in her eyes?"

"No, she—"

"Then it wasn't Marsha. But I've never seen him twice with the same girl on back." Silas stood. "Let me give you a ride home, my dear, since your ride seems to have left in a huff."

As Silas ushered her toward the door, Thea paused. "Do you really think Damon didn't do an adequate job watching the house? Do I need to worry about things missing or broken into?"

"Oh, I very much doubt it," Silas said. "Even such a lackadaisical caretaker is probably passable for Pine Butte. No doubt Dora took that into consideration when she demanded that I hire him."

"Hire him?" Thea asked, surprised. "They were such good friends. Wouldn't he even do *that* for her for free?"

Silas looked pained. "I believe Dora understood the concept of friendship a great deal better than that hoodlum."

Thea wanted to ask more, but Silas opened the door to the street.

When she stepped out of Silas's office, she found Damon leaning against the front of his pickup, talking to a man dressed in motorcycle leathers. As he pushed himself upright, Damon's jeans tightened over his long thigh muscles in a way that drew her gaze. Rebuking herself for even noticing such a thing, she looked quickly up to his face.

Damon introduced the cyclist as Jerry, but Thea only gave him half her attention, for just at that moment, two women emerged from the bank next door to Silas's office, carrying a lockbox and heading for the ATM across the street.

Silas gave them a nod and a smile. "Lovely morning, ladies."

"It is now," Damon agreed, running his blatantly suggestive gaze over the women. "Mmm-hmm," he said as if he were sampling a particularly delicious hot-fudge sundae. "Don't you think so, Jer?"

"You betcha," Jerry agreed obnoxiously.

The older woman shook her head but the younger one giggled as they passed. "He's *such* a hunk," she whispered to her companion.

Thea blushed, remembering how she had stared at Damon's body yesterday. She prayed she hadn't appeared as obvious as this girl.

"He's such a hedonist," said the older woman. "He'll

never grow up. What's he doing hanging out on the street this time of the morning—at his age?''

"Just admiring the view," Damon called to their backs. "Which is just as enticing from this direction, Ida. Age has not dimmed—"

The older woman whirled around. "Damon Free, behave yourself." She spoke with feigned sternness—but even Thea could see her fighting a smile.

Honestly! Did all women of any age react to the man this way? Couldn't they see they were simply encouraging him to flirt! Besides, he was here with Thea.

"Why don't you get a job?" Ida said.

"Job?" Damon put a hand to his throat and spoke as if choking. "You mean...*work*...forty hours a week...*every* week...all year?"

Ida shook her head again and hurried across the street after her friend.

"See what I mean?" Silas spoke in an undertone to Thea.

Thea saw—only too well.

Jerry climbed onto the motorcycle parked next to Damon's truck. "See you, pal." He cocked his head. "Are you riding this afternoon, or do you feel a nagging urge to drop by the job site?"

Damon shrugged. "Hard to tell this early in the day."

"Know what you mean." Jerry laughed and backed his bike out of the space. "Good luck with the heiress."

Heiress? Thea bristled. Did Jerry mean *her*?

Damon glared at his departing friend.

"Damon, what did you say to him?" Thea demanded. "How could you joke about Auntie's estate?"

He brought his stony gaze back to her. "I don't joke about your aunt, Prebble. C'mon, I'll drive you home."

"I shall give Ms. Birch a ride," Silas interjected, reminding Thea of his presence.

Damon flicked one brow up toward his hairline. "Hell you will, Silas." He turned to Thea. "I promised Dora, remember? Now get in the truck...or I'll put you there myself."

Thea narrowed her eyes at him. "You wouldn't dare!"

Something glimmered deep in his eyes. "Try me," he said, his voice silky. His gaze stayed unblinkingly on hers. "Shall I count to three?"

Thea lifted her chin haughtily, but she hurried to the truck.

Without another word, Damon climbed behind the wheel and backed out of the space. He drove at a more reasonable speed than he had on the way into town. His outrageous behavior with those women on Main Street seemed to have eased his impatience. However, the overall mood he'd acquired at Silas's office appeared intact. Preferring silence to another argument, she didn't say a word.

The motion of the truck, the hot air flowing in the windows, her exhaustion from a week of driving and a near-sleepless night, made Thea's lids heavy. She closed her eyes to shield them from the glare of the sun off the dashboard.

The next thing she knew, Damon was shaking her awake in front of Dora's house. Thea blinked up at him. He really was startlingly good-looking, with that smooth dark skin and his full lips and—

He shook her again, more insistently. Suddenly, Thea realized where she was and sat up, pushing his hand off her shoulder.

"Home already?" she said brightly, looking toward the old house with dismay. "I forgot rat poison. I'm sure I heard mice scurrying last night."

"Get a cat," Damon said, reaching across her and opening her door. "You check out the whole house yet? Mice are the least of your worries."

Thea slid out of the truck and turned to snatch her purse off the seat. "I'll look it over from top to bottom when I choose a contractor. I won't be talked out of this, Damon, by a few cracked windows or stained wallpaper." She shut the door.

Damon's curses sounded muffled in the cab. He got out his side and came around the pickup to grab her arm. "I don't know why I give a damn, except for Dora's sake. She wouldn't want you taking this on alone." He propelled her toward the front door. "I'll give you a guided tour of how much you're up against."

"Really, Damon," she said, tugging at her arm, "I'll get a professional restorer to show me—"

"The estimate alone'll cost you more'n this place is worth." He pulled open the screen. "I'll show you enough that you won't want to waste your money."

"What makes you such an expert?" Thea asked.

Damon raked his free hand roughly through his hair. "Brains, Prebble." He pulled her into the house behind him.

Thea followed Damon up the broad staircase. On the landing, he reached toward the window frame and tugged at a corner of the wallpaper. It cracked and little pieces crumbled.

"Wallpaper's all like that," he said. "Dora painted over some, but she didn't replace any. Waiting for little Thea to help pick patterns." He scratched at the wall underneath. "Plaster under here, not Sheetrock."

"I don't suppose the yellow pages abound with plasterers, do they?"

"They charge more than Sheetrockers, too," Damon said. "'Course, you *can* replace plaster with wallboard, especially if you mean to paper over it."

"But...?" Thea asked. "You say 'Sheetrock' the way picnickers say 'ant'."

He let a quick grin flash over his lips. Brief as it was, it transformed his face. No wonder Auntie had been bamboozled by him—so would any woman if he smiled at her all the time.

"That obvious, huh?" Damon said. "Dora said you really wanted to make this B&B historically accurate. Too bad you didn't convince her before she painted over the wainscoting. But at least that can be *un*done. Ripping out the plaster and putting up wallboard will destroy the historical character of this house like nothing else."

"Character versus money," Thea murmured.

"You got it." Damon tapped on a wall, and his fist made a hollow sound. "No insulation under here. Dora's heating bill was astronomical. That's why she closed off so many rooms."

"What kind of heat—"

"Place needs a new furnace, too, or a whole new heating system." He continued up the stairs. "This one'll make it if you decide just to sell the house, but if you really think you can run a business here..."

He let his words trail off and Thea didn't have the energy just then to deny again that she would ever sell Auntie's house. She was already feeling overwhelmed, and she hadn't even gotten to the top of the stairs. Once there, she hesitated, afraid of what she'd feel in Auntie's room.

Damon stopped at the door and looked back at her impatiently. "C'mon, will you? I've got better things to do."

Holding her breath, Thea followed him inside, then exhaled in relief. Like the kitchen, Auntie's room was well kept. Thea knew her aunt had gone to the hospital very early in the morning. Without consciously acknowledging it to herself, she had feared to find evidence of that last night: the bed unmade perhaps, with the indentation of Auntie's head still on the pillow, her slippers on the floor or her old pink cardigan thrown over the back of the chaise.

But, though every place she looked held a memory of Dora, the room was spotless. The bed was made, the drapes were neatly open behind their damask tiebacks, and even the pile of paperbacks Dora always had on her bedside table had been straightened. Except for Dora's knickknacks, every surface was neat and free of clutter. Thea knew Auntie hadn't kept the room this way.

"Who…?"

"The caretaker," Damon said gruffly.

Thea gawked. Obviously, Damon didn't realize she knew he was the caretaker. He might be taking pay, but perhaps he understood more about friendship than Silas comprehended. At least he understood that Dora wouldn't have wanted her untidy room to be seen by anyone else.

"Her workroom was the only place Dora really kept organized."

"I remember," Thea said softly.

"Yeah, well…" Damon lifted one drape away from the wall. "Even in here, the wallpaper needs to be replaced. Crown molding's okay, though, unlike most of the other rooms." He tapped a window sash. "Dora got one of those energy audits from the power company last winter. Every window and door leaked."

"Leaked? You mean rain—"

"Not water," Damon said. "Just air, cold air. When the house was built, heat meant a few more logs on the fire." He shot her a look. "But guests at a B&B'll expect their rooms warm in the mornings."

"I'll only be open in the summer," Thea said.

Damon nodded slowly. "You've forgotten Montana summers? When does summer start in Virginia?"

"Oh, by May it's always hot enough to open the swimming pools," Thea said. "By April it's comfortable. I don't remember ever turning on the heat in April."

"Well, last summer here it snowed on the sixth of July,"

Damon said. "That's unusual but not unheard of. Mornings are always cold in June. And evenings."

"Snow down *here* in July?" Thea asked weakly. "I thought it only snowed in the mountains that late."

Damon rolled his dark eyes. "You're *in* the mountains, Prebble."

Thea looked out the window at the still–snow-covered peaks of the nearest mountains. "Well, that's why people come here, isn't it? To get out of the heat? Feel like they're back in the old West. Rustic living."

"You don't have a chance of pulling this off if you refuse to get your head out of that dreamworld," Damon said, all the impatience back in his voice. "To a tourist, rustic means no traffic and seeing the stars at night. Not freezing his tush on the way to the shower."

Thea nodded, her lips pressed tight in annoyance. Damon might be right about the heat, but he didn't need to speak to her as if she were a slow-witted child. "Fine," she said crisply. "A new furnace, insulation, fix the windows and doors." She cringed inwardly as she asked, "What next?"

"C'mon," Damon said. "This room's nothing."

Thea followed him into the hall.

Damon gestured at the brass wall sconces. "Little cleaning is all these need…"

"Thank heavens." Thea sighed.

"…but the whole house needs to be rewired." Damon hesitated. "Except the cellar. I wired the workroom for Dora a while ago. I don't know why she didn't burn the house down years before." He shook his head. "Fortunately, she didn't use a lot of power tools."

He fiddled with a section of wainscoting till it opened, revealing a hidden drawer. Taking out a key, he turned to one of the closed doors. "Dora kept these rooms locked. She didn't heat them and didn't want the doors opened."

He turned the key, looking grim. "This is where it gets expensive."

Thea swallowed. "Insulating, wiring, heating and new windows aren't expensive?"

"The problem with the windows," Damon said, "is the same as with the floors and moldings in the unused rooms."

When Damon held the door waiting for Thea to enter ahead of him, she heard mice scurrying. Even with sun filtering through the dirty window, the room felt cold. Dust motes swirled everywhere, stirred up by her and Damon's feet. The wallpaper looked dingy and was cracked in places. Worse, the smell of mice permeated the room, and they had left droppings and nests all over.

"Oh, my heavens."

"Forget the mice," Damon said. "Look at the floor." He pointed at dark spots on the wood, strips of the oak flooring that had warped. "These closed-off rooms are the worst, but pieces of it all over the house need to be replaced."

"What about carpeting?" Thea asked.

Damon looked at her as if she'd suggested he eat live worms. "Great idea," he said, sarcasm so sharp in his voice it could cut leather. "Nice and cheap...and *really* historic. How about aluminum siding and AstroTurf for the lawn? Save you a bundle."

Thea wanted so badly to slap him her palm tingled. "Very well, Damon. You made your point. There's no need to be rude."

He nodded curtly. "And all the boards that need replacing are random length."

"'Random' sounds so inaccurate to a C.P.A.," Thea said.

He shook his head. "Actually, replacing random-length boards requires great accuracy." He pointed up. "Like the molding. It's plaster. You can match it with wood, or even Styrofoam."

"Styrofoam?"

"It looks fine painted. But it's all custom work. Whatever yard does it will have to make special knives just to cut your flooring, your trim, your casings."

"Custom means expensive?"

"Very." Damon pointed at the windows. "The panes are not a standard size, so the rails have to be specially cut." He strode over to the window, opened it with less pressure than Thea would have expected. Crooking his finger at her, he sat on the sill and stuck his head outside. "Look up here." His voice sounded far away through the glass.

Uneasy but unwilling to say so, Thea joined him at the window, sliding her head and shoulders out to sit next to him on the sill. She held tight to the inside of the sash, closing her eyes to avoid looking down. Her head began to spin and she gave an involuntary squeal of fear.

In the swirling blackness, she felt Damon's strong warm hand press supportively against her back between her shoulder blades.

"You afraid of heights?" he asked, his tone for once free of scorn or irritation.

"I'm all right," Thea squeaked. Her stomach knotted, and her fingers ached from gripping the sash.

"Yeah, I can tell." He pushed harder on her back as if to reassure her he wouldn't let her go. "If you can't open your eyes, it won't do any good to terrify yourself out here."

Damon slid his hand to her shoulder and pulled her against him. Warmth spread through her and she wanted to curl into the crook of his shoulder, hiding her face there. She knew then she'd be safe.

Safe?

Safe from falling maybe. But safe? Cuddling with Damon Free? The man—the rebel—whose kiss had turned her muscles to mush and made her forget in a few seconds a lifetime of Chelsea's strictures on how not to fall prey to the Prebble flaw. Cuddling with him, for that matter, two floors above the ground in plain sight of whoever drove by up on the road? Insane!

Still, she longed to move her hands from the inside of the window to his waist and cling to him.

Fortunately, she couldn't make herself let go of the sash. She began to tremble.

"C'mon, Prebble," Damon said. "You can see this from the ground."

Thea nodded, her eyes still tightly closed. Slowly, Damon moved his arm, exerting just enough pressure to help her inside without scaring her more. Once she stood again on the solid hardwood floor, she shuddered all over.

Damon regarded her with what looked almost like remorse. "You all right?"

Thea nodded, feeling silly now that it was over. "I don't usually...lose it like that."

"Dora was that way about heights, too." Damon watched her for a few more seconds while the sardonic mask slowly returned to his face. "Maybe you got more from her than the wild streak."

"I do *not* have the—"

"Ri-ight," he interrupted, disbelief clear in his tone. "Let's go downstairs." He gestured at the room. "You've seen enough here."

Thea put a hand to her head, which was still spinning. "I'm not sure I can take in any more today, Damon."

"You need to see the outside, Prebble. Get a grip." He took her hand and led her toward the stairs, but released her to descend.

Resigned, Thea trailed downstairs after him and out to the front yard. He pointed to the gables.

"See the siding that looks like concrete?"

Thea squinted in the sunlight.

"It's canvas. Authentically historic."

Surprised, Thea transferred her gaze to Damon. He actually sounded interested in this part of the house. "Doesn't it leak?"

"Nope, not after it's primed. That canvas up there has lasted over a century. It still doesn't leak, but the paint's failed, so it needs to be replaced."

"I've never heard of it," Thea said. "It sounds like…a tent."

"Exactly." He shot her his pedantic look. "Haven't you ever felt warm and dry in a tent in the rain?"

"Actually—" Thea bit her lip "—I've never been camping."

Damon stared. "You're kidding."

"Chelsea didn't think it was proper," Thea said defensively. "You know, boys and girls sleeping that close to each other without walls and doors."

Damon rolled his eyes. "Does this Chelsea chick have any kids of her own?"

Thea shook her head.

"Figures," he muttered. "Probably never learned how."

"Damon!" Thea protested. "Weren't you telling me about canvas?"

"Right." He looked back up at the gable. "It's like everything else in the house. You can replace it with siding, but if you stick with historical accuracy…"

"It costs more," Thea said grimly.

"You got it." He pointed at the upper floors. "The new roof and paint will be standard items. But…" He shot her a glance. "Painting'll cost more, too, since you'll have to hire it done. I doubt you'd be much good on an extension ladder.''

Thea looked at Damon's big tan hands, resting lightly on his hips, his wide shoulders beneath the chambray shirt he'd donned to go to Silas's office, his long, powerful legs beneath the black denim. Every inch of him looked strong, capable, she was sure, of somehow handling all the disasters he was telling her about.

But Thea didn't feel that way at all. She felt as if she'd stepped into a puddle of quicksand that was pulling her down fast and hard. It felt almost as if Damon was in league with Father...and J. P. Crawford. That thought brought a little straightness back to her spine.

Maybe Damon was exaggerating. After all, just because he did a little construction work, that didn't make him an expert. Maybe someone else would see ways to cut costs somehow.

Besides, Damon's old animosities toward Thea didn't make him the best judge of whether she could stay here and make the B&B a success. Everything he'd said and done since she arrived made it clear that he thought she ought to sell out and go home. Now that she thought about it, he hadn't behaved all that differently on her last visit to Pine Butte.

"What makes you so sure about all this, Damon?" she asked.

He walked over and stood in front of her, shading the sun from her eyes and casting his face in shadow. "Which part do you think I'm lying about?" he challenged.

"Oh, not lying," Thea hastened to assure him. "I just wonder...well, I'm an accountant. We believe in checking—"

"You don't believe me?" Damon's tone didn't betray any emotion, but his hands on his hips curled into fists.

"Call Marsha at the lumberyard, ask her. She'll tell you—she gave Dora a bid a few months ago."

"Is hers the only lumberyard in town?"

"Only, best, cheapest," Damon said. "Call around, check that, too, if you want. Then when you can't find any more excuses to ignore reality—" he aimed a thumb at her Corvette "—pack your sh—stuff back in your hot car and drive home to Daddy. Silas will handle the sale for you."

With a disgusted oath, he turned on his heel, strode to his pickup and jerked open the door. Thea watched him, all her uncertainties hardening into resolve. Maybe, just maybe, if he hadn't made that last crack about "Daddy", reminding her too forcefully of what awaited her if she failed here, she might have listened to him.

She stood and raised her voice to an almost unladylike level. "No one will handle the sale for me, Damon. I'm not selling!"

Stepping into his pickup, Damon froze and glared at her over the roof of the cab. "Damn Prebble women," he muttered. "You got all Dora's stubbornness. Too bad you didn't get her good sense! If you can find someone to fix this monstrosity—" he waved a hand angrily at her house "—at a price you can afford, I'll kiss your a—"

"Damon!" Thea exclaimed.

"Ah, hell!" Damon slid into his truck and sped up Dora's drive.

CHAPTER FOUR

THEA sat on the step, staring disconsolately at the Corvette Damon had sneered at: red and sleek and dustier than it ever got in the city. The car had been a gift from her family when she passed the C.P.A. exam on her first try.

Father rarely did anything so ostentatious. He was an army officer through and through, and he knew that uniformity was an important part of the military life. He lived on his army pay and never complained about it. He could undoubtedly have called on his family, just as Dora could have called on the Prebbles, if he'd ever needed to. But as far as Thea knew, he never had. Until the Corvette.

The whole Birch clan had presented her with the car. Which was why she'd been *so* thrilled when Father handed her the keys. She'd felt truly accepted into the fold that day, as if she had finally overcome the stain of being half-Prebble.

The Prebbles might be "old money"—which Thea had come to learn usually meant not much was left—and the Birches merely upstarts, but at least Birches didn't get pregnant out of wedlock, or worse, get married six times to bedroom-eyed husbands barely out of their teens. Obviously, the Birches believed Thea had escaped the "Prebble flaw" that caused such wild behavior, or they wouldn't have given her a gift that seemed to tempt it.

Shaking off her musings, Thea went inside to call this Marsha person and find out what she was really up against. Just as she reached for the phone, it rang. Thea glared at it.

She didn't need to pick it up to know it was Father. Who

else knew she was here? Besides, she'd agreed to call him after the will reading. The bell jangled again.

Steeling herself, Thea picked up the receiver. If she didn't talk to him now, he'd just call later.

"Hello, Theadora," Norman said crisply. "I trust you got through the will reading like a Birch?"

"Like a Birch, Father?"

"You know what I mean," Norman said. "No unseemly displays of emotion."

Thea thought of Damon's outburst, sure Father would have considered it an "ill-bred exhibition". But she purposely didn't mention it—baiting Father was the last thing she needed to do right now.

"No, Father, of course I kept my control."

The point in each conversation when Thea quit talking and just agreed with everything Father said seemed to occur earlier and earlier. She had an uneasy feeling he meant to call her every day to remind her how the family would feel about having an innkeeper in its ranks.

Today, she was able to hurry him off the phone because he had a meeting to attend at the Pentagon. She said little until he offered to send J.P. out to help her with the sale of the house. At that, she grew quite adamant. Whatever her decision about Auntie's house, Thea knew she had to make it soon, or so many pushy males would descend on her, she wouldn't stand a chance.

A quick smile crossed her face as she imagined Damon's reaction to J.P.'s phony self-importance. That would be a confrontation worth watching. But not one she had any intention of risking.

After she got Father off the phone, Thea looked up the number of the lumberyard and dialed.

"Pine Butte Lumber," a harried female voice answered.

Thea could hardly think over the distracting background noises. A radio station played not quite loudly enough to drown out several male voices and some sort of machine noise.

"Is this Marsha?" Thea asked.

"You got her," Marsha said. "What can I do for you?"

Thea identified herself, then continued, "I understand from Damon Free that you made a bid for my aunt a few months ago on the cost of restoring her house. I was wondering—"

"Lemme get to my office." Marsha abruptly put Thea on hold.

Thea tapped her pen against her teeth as she waited, listening to loud cowboy music on the hold switch.

"Yeah, now what about that bid?"

"Well, I'd like to know the amount. Damon just gave me a rundown on how much needs to be done here," Thea said, "and I have to make some hard decisions."

"No kidding," Marsha said. "Hang on."

This time, she didn't bother to push the hold button. Thea could hear papers rustling, file-cabinet drawers opening and closing, and Marsha's mutterings.

"Here it is," Marsha said. "Now, you understand, this is just for materials, and it's only for Damon."

"Pardon me?" Thea asked. "What do you mean, 'for Damon'? I thought it was for me. My house. My aunt's house. Damon's just—"

"Don't get huffy," Marsha said. "God, you're just like he said you'd be. What d'ya think, you can do the work yourself?"

Thea swallowed her impulse to bristle at Marsha's words. "No, of course I plan to hire someone, but certainly not Damon Free. He's just a construction worker and not a very dedicated one as far as I can tell."

"Yeah, how can you tell that?" Marsha snapped. "You only been here a few days, right?"

"Only one, but I—"

"Exactly." Marsha gave an exasperated sigh. "So who the hell d'ya plan to hire?"

"I don't know yet," Thea said. "I don't know anyone in Pine Butte and—"

"My point," Marsha said. "If you hire someone besides Damon, he'll see different things need fixing. They always do. So the bid'll change. I can only guarantee this for Damon. Now, ya got a problem with that?"

"My problem is getting my house restored properly."

"Well, trust me, Damon's perfectly capable."

Thea felt as if Marsha was selling her Damon along with flooring and insulation. And why would Marsha care? Perhaps she could only count on getting the order if Damon got the job, or perhaps…

Thea couldn't help remembering Silas's warning that Marsha had personal feelings for Damon. How had he phrased it? That when Marsha recommended Damon, Thea should think hard about what Marsha really thought Damon did so well. But Marsha sounded like a hardheaded businesswoman. Would she really let that sort of thing influence her *this* much?

Papers rattled again. "This figure doesn't include subs either. Just for materials, it'll run you $154,776 and—"

"And eighty-four cents?" Thea said in a dazed tone.

"Yeah, how'd you know?"

Disoriented, Thea put her free hand to her head, feeling as if it were swirling. One hundred fifty-four thousand seven hundred seventy-six dollars? The exact amount of Damon's bequest—the bequest he'd turned down. Auntie must have meant the money for the house. But why would she leave it to Damon instead of Thea? *He* had no interest in seeing Dora's house restored. What *had* Dora been thinking?

"Just a lucky guess," she said to Marsha, confusion making her voice squeak.

Marsha hesitated a second. "So you get someone else, have him bring me his list, I'll give him another bid. It'll be higher, because prices are going up. And it'll be damn tough to find a contractor available. Most of 'em only like new construction, and besides, they're all booked up for the summer."

"It's only May," Thea said.

"A contractor who doesn't have his summer scheduled to the last day by now, that's not somebody you want to hire. But why bother anyway? Damon Free's a helluva builder. And he knows the house."

A builder? Damon? Just because he worked... "worked"?...a little construction?

Thea thought of him lounging around downtown with that other biker, joking about whether to bother to drop by his job that day. He'd told her himself he was only working a little construction on the beach. That didn't sound like the sort of worker she wanted to engage for a major job like this restoration.

On the other hand, at the moment Thea didn't even know the *name* of a contractor. Of course, she could probably get a name or two from Silas, but she doubted Silas had the same vision of the house that she did. But, oddly, Damon did. He knew it and seemed to love it, she thought, from the way he'd spoken about it this afternoon.

Thea winced at the memory of that conversation. Even if she wanted to hire Damon, it seemed unlikely he'd be willing to work for her anyway.

"Thing is," Marsha continued when Thea didn't say anything, "I can't hold these prices much longer for you, either. It's almost summer, building season. Prices'll start going up for me, too, end of this month. If ya wanna go ahead, tell me now."

"Now?" Her earlier squeak was nothing compared to this one.

Marsha clicked something against the phone. "Now or…few more days maybe. Not more." She exhaled loudly and Thea realized she must be smoking.

"I haven't even spoken to Damon," Thea said. "We don't exactly…see eye to eye on things." She groaned inwardly at the thought of trying to persuade Damon to take on this job. "Don't I need to get some sort of written agreement from him?"

"Nah," Marsha said. "Not if you order this stuff from his estimate. He'll live up to his word."

Thea felt as if she was making a major decision with only half the facts. But one thing she knew for certain: if she had even a prayer of getting her house fixed, she had to take Marsha's deal—Damon and all. Because she didn't dare let her costs go up another penny. Despite Marsha's encouraging words about Damon, Thea had an idea she was going to have to do some major groveling to convince him.

"What will I do with all the stuff?" she asked weakly.

"Damon fixed Dora's barn last year—the roof leaked," Marsha said. "You can store the materials out there and I can keep some here. But I've got to get my suppliers going on this."

Fixed the barn? That certainly had a positive ring to it.

Thea sighed gustily. The pressure Marsha was putting on her was more immediate than Father's, more direct. But in fact, Marsha was only pushing Thea to do something she wanted to do anyway.

Agreeing to this astronomical purchase would lock Thea into the restoration. Even Father would see that. She hoped.

Just minutes ago, he'd ordered her to make no decisions without his guidance. But hadn't she come west for that very purpose? To make her *own* decisions? She didn't need Father's input nor, heaven forbid, J.P.'s.

Thea thought of J.P. in this beautiful, pristine place, in one of Auntie's beds between her silky, old-fashioned per-

cale sheets. She thought of his clumsy, loathsome, mani-
cured hands, of his ego...which would undoubtedly be the
first thing in the valley larger than Mount Anthony.

"I'll do it, Marsha," Thea said. "Please go ahead with
the order."

"Orders," Marsha corrected her. "I'll send you a couple
copies of this bid. I've signed it as a not-to-exceed price,
which I'm only giving you because of Damon."

Oh, of course, Thea thought, rankled by Marsha's con-
tinual devotion to Damon. *What on earth does the man do
to her? Whatever it is, it must still be going on or surely a
woman as strong as this Marsha wouldn't be prattling on
about him the way she did.*

"Please sign the extra copy and send it back to me. I
need to protect myself on an order this big."

"I won't change my mind," Thea said. "I can come in
and sign it if you wish. We should probably meet if we're
going to be working together."

"We'll meet soon enough, I'm sure," Marsha said. "But
for now, I'll just stick this in the mail." She exhaled again.
"Be talking to you."

Thea replaced the receiver, sure Marsha was right—
they'd be speaking again. She wasn't terribly comfortable
with that idea. It was quite obvious Marsha still had strong
feelings for Damon, and it made Thea ill at ease to discuss
his merits knowing that.

Especially since Damon had made no effort to hide *his*
interest in other women. Thea had an urge to call Marsha
back and tell her about the beautiful brunette she'd seen
clinging to Damon on his motorcycle, then ask her if she
still recommended him so highly.

Of course, she'd never really do such a thing because
the ensuing discussion would be excruciatingly embarrassing. If she succeeded in hiring Damon, he was going to be

around all summer. That would be hard enough without having very personal knowledge about him.

It *was* hard having him around, Thea admitted that. Something about the man disturbed her carefully controlled equilibrium. She wandered into the kitchen and spied her sandalwood recipe box. Auntie had made it for her years ago from an antique tea caddy.

It was filled with over seven hundred recipes and patterns for the B&B. All kinds of breakfast breads and rolls, egg dishes, even a recipe for mints to put on the pillows at night. Curtain patterns, slipcovers, Victorian-style and prairie dresses, stenciling patterns for walls, furniture and drapes. Thea had been collecting them since she was thirteen years old.

Putting her hand on the lid of the box, she let all those dreams fill her with determination now. She could handle working in close proximity with Damon; she could overcome pressure from her family; she could find a way to pay for this massive project. She would not let anything deter her.

With a new sense of conviction, Thea moved her things from the den and the rest of her luggage from the car up to Auntie's room. The room had the Dora look Thea remembered: lots of sunshine, a puffy yellow quilt and cheery wallpaper with bright yellow flowers growing up a white trellis.

Of course, the quilt had grown rather flat over the years, and both it and the wallpaper had faded. But Thea could still picture Auntie sitting on the yellow cushions in the window seat, looking across the lake at her beloved mountains.

The sound of mice scratching across the hall brought Thea out of her memories with a shiver of revulsion. Mice! Right across the hall from her bedroom.

She felt imprisoned in the few rooms Auntie had lived

in. And Thea couldn't stomach the thought of putting rat poison in Auntie's bedroom nor, heaven knows, in the kitchen. Maybe Damon was right for once. She ought to get a cat.

The next afternoon, Thea returned from Bozeman and put the cat carrier down in the living room. "Now be good, kitties," she said as she opened the wire door, "and chase the mice right out of here."

Slowly, two beautiful black Persian kittens emerged from the carrying box. There had been cheaper cats at the pet store, but Thea had bonded with these immediately. Sniffing the air with their pushed-in noses, their green eyes alert to their new surroundings, they mewed curiously.

After making a careful tour of the living room, the kittens slunk out to the entry hall, wiggling their noses like crazy. A mousy noise upstairs caught their attention, and within seconds they were streaking up the stairs as silently as cats can.

Damon Free pounded on the screen door. Seeing her inside, he opened the door and marched up to her. "What the hell have you done now?" he demanded furiously.

Thea was taken aback. "Pardon me?"

"Don't give me that," he said, jabbing a finger at her. "I just talked to Marsha. She said you're 'hiring' me to restore your house!"

"Yes, um..." Thea's throat closed. All the logical arguments she'd prepared last night left her brain in the face of his anger. "That's right, I did. I—"

"Oh, you did?" Damon said. "How did you do that exactly? Talk to my agent? I mean, did it ever occur to you to give me a call first?"

"Well, actually, Damon, yes, it did." Thea's words came out choppily, but not quite stuttering. She wished he'd step back a few feet. "I mentioned that to Marsha. I'm sure she told you. About calling you and, well, about maybe needing something in writing. But she said—''

"And what the hell made you think Marsha could answer for me?''

"I, um…''

Damon had a point. An unanswerable point as far as Thea was concerned, but she hoped not to let him know that.

"Do you know what you've done?''

"I do know that, yes,'' Thea said. "Whether or not you take this job. I've ordered the materials to fix up the house. I will pay for that with—''

"I know how you'll pay for that, Prebble,'' Damon said, obviously exasperated. "Didn't you wonder at all when you heard the amount of the bid?''

"It confused me,'' Thea said. "I don't know why Auntie did that, left that money to you instead of to me, when it's obvious what she wanted it used for. Anyway, that's what I decided to do with it. After all, I'll inherit it now, and I'll spend it just as she—''

"What if I change my mind?'' Damon asked. "I haven't signed anything yet.''

Thea felt a lump of lead settle in her stomach. "You mean, keep the money? And spend it on…something else?''

"I could.''

"But…will you?''

Damon turned away, expelling an oath. "No, dammit. If I took it, I'd just spend it on the same damn fool thing you're spending it on.'' He whirled on her. "Which was why I didn't take it in the first place! Because I'd be committed to this insane project.''

"You sound just like Father.''

"Well, I hate to agree with the old fart, but this time he's right.''

Thea bit her lip. She should defend Father, but she wanted to get to the real point of this discussion. "You mean you won't take the job, Damon?" For some reason, that thought seemed to deplete a great part of her enthusiasm.

He put a foot up on the bench very close to her thigh. "Take the money, Thea, sell the house and go home."

She spoke to his bent knee. "I am home, Damon. I've spent thirteen years dreaming about this B&B, with Dora and alone. I've moved all over the world, but I've never found a place that felt as much like home as this house does."

Feeling oppressed by Damon's intense, looming presence, Thea stood and took a few steps away. "I've thought and thought about what's missing at all those cold hotels and army billets. I want to make everyone who stays here feel he's found a home away from home that he can come back to year after—"

"Earth to Thea," Damon interrupted, turning to face her. "Quit dreaming and join us in reality, will you?"

Thea regarded him, the tension in his shoulders and back, his clenched fists. "I don't understand why you're so angry. Marsha didn't seem to think you'd have a problem with this job. Obviously *Dora* thought you should do the project. That's why she left you the money. She said so in that letter—that she saw good in this for you."

"Forget it, Prebble. You don't know what you're talking about."

She lifted her chin slightly. "A paying job isn't all that bad. You might get to like it. It might even improve your reputation."

For some reason, instead of making Damon angrier, Thea's insult made him smile. Just a slow curving of his lips, a flash of straight white teeth and a warming of those charcoal-dark eyes. Thea couldn't help smiling back, couldn't help wishing Damon reacted to everything she said with a smile like that.

His next words jarred her back to the present. "You don't get it, do you?" he said. "Dora thought that doing this restoration would be *so* good for my reputation that it would be worth it to me to do it for nothing, to donate my time. That's why she left me the money for the materials."

Thea's jaw dropped. "You're kidding. Why on earth would Auntie expect you to do so much for free?"

Damon's eyes seemed to shutter over. "I would have done it for her for nothing. I...owed her. I'd never have charged her a nickel." He flicked up one of his dark, expressive brows in that way Thea was beginning to find as annoying as a mosquito. "But I'll charge you, Prebble. Full price."

"Well, of *course* I mean to hire you, Damon. How could you think otherwise?" She folded her hands in front of her. "'The laborer is worthy of his hire.'"

"And do you have any idea what that kind of 'laborer' costs?" His tone made her squirm. "Construction pricing ever come up in your accounting work?"

Damon's excessive sarcasm sent anxious signals up and down Thea's nerves. "How much are you talking about, Damon? Quit taunting and tell me a price."

"With the materials, by the time you're finished, you'll have over three hundred in the place. Maybe quite a bit over. It'll depend some on the subcontractors." Damon sounded completely assured, even unconcerned, about what he was saying.

Thea thought she might faint. She grabbed one of the oak coat hooks on the hall tree to steady herself. "Three hundred *thousand* dollars?"

"Right." Damon's smile this time was so cynical, Thea hoped she'd never see it again. "That's a fair price for restoration—more than fair. Ask anyone."

"Oh, dear Lord." She slumped back onto the bench. "Oh, no. Oh, my."

"I thought you'd see the light," Damon said. "So better take that one hundred and fifty, slap a coat of paint on the place and sell it as is."

"I can't. I've already committed to Marsha, told her to go ahead."

Damon gestured toward the den. "Get on the phone quick and tell her—".

"I can't," Thea stopped him. "She called this morning to tell me everything was on order. She faxed all her suppliers right after our phone call yesterday—to lock in the old prices."

"And lock in *me*!" Damon growled.

Turning away from her, he strode to the door and glared out, bracing himself with a fist on either side of the jamb. Thea couldn't actually hear him swearing, but she was sure he was doing so mentally.

"Damon," Thea said, "*you're* not locked in. I only committed myself."

"Like hell!" he growled, without turning around. "I gave my word."

"Your word?" His spine stiffened when she spoke. "To whom? Certainly not to me."

"To Dora, to Marsha..." He shook his head. "That's *my* bid you ordered from."

"But—"

Damon faced her, his full lips hardened into a tight, grim line. "We're stuck with it," he said, sounding as much resigned as angry. "So unless you've got three hundred grand lying around, you'd better phone Daddy and get him to fork over some of his tightly held cash."

"Oh, I couldn't, no indeed," Thea said fiercely. Damon's words snapped her out of her shock, reminding her how much this project meant to her. "Not Father. He agrees with you that the project is insane. Crazy. Tainted with the...'flaw'.'' Her voice shook and rose several decibels. "He thinks I'll return home as soon as I can sell the house and contents, go back to my sensible, boring career and marry that—" She slapped a hand over her mouth, blushing furiously at what she'd said.

Damon chuckled and walked slowly toward her. "What's the matter, Prebble?" he asked softly. "Don't like Daddy's choice?"

Thea shuddered at the memory of how much she loathed J.P.'s touch. "I make my own choices in such matters," she lied. "And I do not choose to marry *anyone*."

She closed her eyes, unwilling to meet Damon's penetrating gaze. Even blind, she knew when he stood right in front of her.

Damon curled a finger under her chin and lifted. "Not anyone?"

His touch was gentle. Thea's cheeks were on fire and she kept her eyes tightly closed.

"The way I remember it," he said, his voice silky, "you liked that marriage kind of stuff a lot—you know, kissing, touching..."

His hand slid softly over her heated cheek to the back of her neck, gently urging her up off the bench toward him.

Though his touch contained no hint of actual force, Thea had to struggle to resist it.

Usually, this sort of situation caused her no problem. Of course, *usually* men didn't touch her without her permission. She had learned in college how to give signals that let men know *she* would decide when touching would begin. Despite all her practice, however, Damon didn't seem any better at reading her signals now than he did when she was seventeen.

Or had she quit sending them? She didn't, after all, find his touch repulsive...quite the reverse in fact. Which was all the more reason to get her signals back in operating order. For this weakening of her resolve could only mean that the "Prebble flaw" Damon found so amusing—and that she had spent so many years successfully eradicating from her personality—had clicked into gear the moment she'd encountered this dark-eyed, silky-voiced, soft-lipped...

Thea rose and stepped away, putting needed space between them. "No, Damon. I know what you're talking about. Don't think I've forgotten. I learned a valuable lesson from you that day. It is *not* a lesson I need to have repeated." She pointed a finger at him, furious to see her hand shaking. "I do not permit such situations to occur anymore. I know the signs, believe me, and I know to avoid them."

Before she could react, Damon grabbed the hand she extended toward him and gave a tug. Her resistance failed entirely and she stumbled into his chest. Capturing her other hand, he held them both tightly in the small of her back, pressing her to him. The warmth of his body flowed into hers, creating a melting puddle of heaviness low in her belly.

Staring up at his laughing, ironic look, she realized she was out of breath...or perhaps Damon was holding her so tightly she couldn't breathe. Whichever, she definitely needed more oxygen.

And she definitely ought to do something about his embrace. But she couldn't. Damon's heat did something strange to her, something she couldn't fight, for it seemed to drain her strength.

Damon chuckled his warm, satisfied male chuckle. "Did you see this one coming, Prebble? You didn't do much to avoid it—or do you want it, too?" His head dipped toward hers.

"Of course not," Thea said, fighting to restore reason to her brain. "Release me at once."

She squirmed in his arms, which made her even more aware of how good it felt to be held by a man like Damon—a real man. Not one of those stuffy three-piece suits Father approved of, or that horrible J.P. who just wanted to grab and never stopped talking about himself long enough to really kiss a woman properly.

Good heavens, *what* was she thinking?

Thea pulled out of Damon's arms and stepped back, bumping into the banister. With a wobble and a gasp, she plopped down on the curved bottom stair.

Afraid to acknowledge how useless her defenses seemed against Damon, Thea changed the subject as thoroughly as she could. "Since Father thinks," she said breathlessly, "I've come here to sell the house, I can't ask him for money. I wouldn't anyway. He thinks this B&B is the sort of wild thing Mama or Dora would do. He would only give me money if I said I couldn't get the house ready to sell without it."

"In other words," Damon said in that disrespectful tone he used when speaking of Father, "if you take his money, you have to do exactly what he says."

"Not exactly," Thea said. "But...I think he's afraid if I stay here, I'll turn out like my mother. She was so like Dora, that after she stayed here with Auntie, she ran off with—"

"I know your mother," Damon said. "She's not much like Dora at all."

"You know my mother?" Startled, Thea stood, though her knees wobbled.

"She visits every time she gets a new husband." Damon sounded mildly scornful, but not nearly as judgmental as Father and Chelsea always did. "She's witty and sexy and likes men. Dora might have been like that when she was young. But in terms of loyalty, generosity, love—your mother doesn't come close to Dora.''

Thea stared at Damon slack-jawed. He seemed suddenly to realize that he was revealing as much about himself as he was about the two women he was talking about. The shutters fell over his eyes again and his face turned impassive.

"Anyway, Prebble," he said, his voice icy cold as if he was furious with her for prying these revelations out of him, "your father's right. Sell the place." Damon strode the length of the entry hall and left, slamming the door behind him.

Thea stood, clinging to the banister, with the same feeling she always had when Damon left. As if a storm had just passed over. This time, the feeling was even more intense.

His parting pronouncement that he knew her mother left Thea nearly dizzy with confusion. The way he talked, it sounded as if he knew her mother better than Thea did herself.

Not that *that* was difficult. Thea hadn't seen much of her mother the past twelve years. Letters and phone calls, lunches when Mother came to town with a new husband.

Thea had always found it hard to have a personal conversation with Mother because they were never alone. The last two husbands Harriet had shown up with had only been a few years older than Thea. How could she pour out her innermost feelings with a twenty-five-year-old bedroom-eyed Frenchman kissing her mother's hand and cheek during the entire lunch?

Last time had been right in the middle of the Quad at graduate school. Thea's friends had all wanted to know who that gorgeous man was. Admitting René was her stepfather ranked high on Thea's list of most embarrassing moments.

On top of that, there was Damon's unsympathetic description of the harrowing financial predicament she'd gotten herself into. Three hundred and something thousand dollars!

Thea leaned against the newel post, rubbing her temples. She would spend her inheritance, not just the bequest Damon had turned down—any other cash in the estate. She could draw out her retirement money and the rest of her savings, most of which were graduation gifts from relatives. She could—Thea swallowed hard—sell her Corvette, sell Father's family's car and explain to him that she had done it to put the money into the B&B he thought absolute madness, and...

And she'd *still* be thousands short. Tens of thousands.

Thea thought of all the times she'd told clients, "Diversify. Don't put all your eggs in one basket." Yet here she was counting on this house, this dream of a B&B, to rescue her from a stultifying job, a confining family, and worst of all...J.P. All her eggs in one basket? All her dreams, as well.

And now to bring her dream to life, she'd hired a man she couldn't afford, whose only recommendation came from his lover and who, as far as Thea knew, had never handled this kind of job before!

Had she truly, as Father thought, lost all her senses when it came to this project?

Thea walked out onto the porch and down the steps. Turning, she looked back up at the house she loved. In her mind's eye, she saw a hand-carved sign swinging from the porch beam: Dora's Historic Bed and Breakfast.

Thea would find a way. She had to. She just didn't quite know how...yet.

CHAPTER FIVE

THEA sat cross-legged on the front steps with a sketch pad in her lap. When she was growing up, Father had always told her that since she wasn't creative—to which he usually added, "Thank God!" since so many of Mother's young lovers and husbands were artists—she'd have to do something useful with her life. He'd helped her choose accounting.

It was only Auntie Dora who had ever encouraged her to draw. It was one of the reasons Thea hadn't gone down to Auntie's workroom yet—she knew finding some of her childish drawings framed and hanging on the wall would reduce her to tears.

Hoping to dispel the discouragement she felt after Damon's visit, Thea sketched the sign she had in mind. On one side of the page, she drew a prim Victorian lady in a lacy high-necked dress with big, puffed leg-of-mutton sleeves. On the other side, the lady's guest: a nineteenth-century gold miner, bearded, long-haired, dressed in fringed buckskins. Between them they held the sign: Auntie Dora's B&B.

She grinned as she added a second line: Baths—10 Cents.

Thea had almost relaxed when the roar of Damon's pickup sounded as he sped back down Dora's drive toward her. Spinning the truck around in front of the house, he stuck his head out the window and hollered.

"You *do* know you've got to get a business license to turn this place into a bed-and-breakfast, don't you?"

"I do?" Thea looked up from her sketch pad. "Why didn't you tell me before, Damon?"

"I didn't hire on as your nanny, Prebble. I figured a good look at the place would bring you back to reality." He rolled his eyes. "Should've known better."

"Well, I can't imagine I'll have any problem getting a license."

"Your imagination needs exercise then," he said, turning off the ignition. "All the land around the lake—" he gestured toward the water "—was zoned residential last year."

"I thought it wasn't even in city limits."

"It's not," he said. "But the county delegated it to the city, and you can't run a business here without a variance of the zoning laws. Trust me, you won't get it."

Thea pursed her lips. "Well, for heaven's sake, why not? I'm going to turn a ramshackle old dwelling into a beautifully restored historically significant B&B." She stood. "You're just grasping at straws, Damon." She shook a finger at him. "Many people find a full-time job quite satisfying, you know. You might—"

"What the hell is that?" Damon interrupted, pointing at something behind her. He opened the door and climbed out of the truck.

Thea looked over her shoulder. "That's Lady Macbeth, a Persian cat." She put down her pad to pick up the kitten.

"I *know* it's a cat, for God's sake." Damon came closer, glaring at the kitten. "What is it doing here?"

"I bought her...and her sister, Lizzie Borden. They're to kill the mice."

"Now there's a revelation."

Thea pursed her lips at Damon's look. "I got a good deal."

"Two bits ain't a good deal for a cat," he said. "You can always get one for free. Barn cats that know what to do with mice." His eyes narrowed at the creature in Thea's arms. "How much did you pay?"

Thea's cheeks warmed under his scrutiny. The difference between two bits and $350 was so great, she couldn't get the words out.

"Really, Damon," she managed, "I don't believe I need your permission to buy pets."

Damon lifted a brow at her glowing cheeks. "You paid a bundle, didn't you? Over a hundred? You got cheated." Absently, he scratched the kitten behind the ears and it began to purr. "You'll never get this house done if you don't get over that Daddy's-little-princess approach to life."

"That is *not* my approach to life, and—"

"And another thing," he said, stroking Lady down her back. "You'll have to do some of the work, the easy stuff, like stripping paint."

"Ugh," Thea said with feeling. "I used to strip furniture for Auntie. I hate those fumes."

The smile Damon gave her did not reassure. "The fumes won't bother you nearly as much as your boss."

"Boss?"

"Me. Don't you get it? If you actually get a license for this place, which I seriously doubt, you'll be taking orders from me for the next six months." He took a step closer and leaned over her. "Get used to it."

"I…" Thea stared up at him, wanting to put her hand on his chest and push him back a few steps. But she knew better than to voluntarily put a hand anywhere on Damon. The powerful pull her body always felt toward his would easily overcome the lesser force—her resistance. Thank heavens she had the cat in her hands.

"Better give it some thought, Prebble. Then call Marsha and see how to get out of this. I bet she can turn off most of those orders for a ten percent restocking fee."

"Ten percent?" Thea wailed. "You mean pay her over fifteen thousand dollars for *nothing*? Never!"

He shook his head. "You don't have a clue what you're getting into." He glanced at her Corvette as he walked toward his pickup. "The cats'll look great in your car—both useless." He pulled open his truck door.

"I plan to sell that car, Damon. I'm in the market for a...clunker. Please let me know if you hear about one."

Damon frowned at her. "That how you plan to pay me, Prebble? Selling off bits of your life?"

"It's better than mortgaging the land." Thea lifted her chin. "Besides, it's my life, not yours."

He regarded her for a long minute. "You're right," he said at last. "Why should I give a damn?"

Despite his last remark, Damon looked disturbed when he drove off.

Thea sat at her computer, mulling over her letter to the variance committee. She'd called the Town Hall early this morning and learned Damon was right about the zoning ordinance. But the clerk had been frustratingly vague about procedures.

"Oh, just write a letter to the city council," she'd said. "I mean, it's not as though they don't know where Dora Prebble's place is and all."

"Just a letter?" Thea persisted. "From me, not my lawyer? Don't they want to see a copy of the will, so they'll know the house is mine?"

"Oh, everyone knows that," the clerk said.

This casual small-town approach to business was very appealing, but it made Thea a little uneasy. "What do I need to cover in the letter?"

"Well, Dora didn't take such good care of it the last years, did she?" the clerk said. "So you better say what you mean to do to the house and who's gonna do it, you know? So the councilmen know you're really gonna bring it up to code before they grant the variance.''

"Does the council grant it?'' Thea said. "I thought it was the variance committee.''

"The council has final say, but they always go along with the recommendation of the committee.''

The conversation left Thea wondering how much detail to include in her request. Should she just tell the council that she planned to restore the house to its original form? Or did they want to know all that Damon had told her about canvas and floorboards and wallpaper? No, better just to say her contractor had made a detailed estimate.

When the letter was typed and signed, Thea made out a grocery list that included more cleaning products than food. Locking the door behind her, she left for town. As she crested the hill at the end of Dora's drive, she stopped to look around. Ahead of her, down the other side of the hill, houses filled what used to be empty pasture. They were good-size, not close together, with lovely views of the lake.

But nothing like Dora's, which would always remain hidden in its own draw. Dora's land, now hers, continued right down to the shoreline, so no one could ever build in front of her. And the hillside in back of the house was covered in evergreens. No wonder Dora had never wanted to go back to Boston.

After dropping off her letter, Thea stopped at the grocery store where Auntie had always done business. She parked next to a motorcycle, wondering if it belonged to Damon. It was hard to tell—motorcycles all looked alike.

Inside, she began filling her cart, absently listening to the owner of the store, whose booming voice could be heard all over the store welcoming customers. He seemed to know and like everyone who bought from him, so when his loud voice suddenly turned cold and angry, Thea was surprised.

She was just wheeling her full basket toward the checkout counter when she saw whom the grocer was talking to: Damon.

"I might have known," the grocer said nastily, "that a special on beer'd bring *you* in here."

Thea's jaw dropped. This was the man she'd heard greeting his customers as if each one was his best friend?

"You got that straight, Mel," Damon said, his voice sneering. "Couldn't pass it up. Enlarged the box on my bike just to hold twelve-packs."

"I oughta refuse you," Mel growled. "I'm probably liable, like a bartender."

"Ri-ight." Damon's voice dripped sarcasm. "Picked up two or three times a week for drunk driving, that's me."

The lovely long-legged brunette Thea had seen on the back of Damon's motorcycle that first day came out of the room behind the cash registers. "Oh, Dad, for heaven's sake, just sell him the beer."

"Roni," Mel growled at her, "don't tell me—"

Roni nudged her father and pointed at Thea and the others who had stopped to watch. "People are listening."

With an unintelligible grumble, Mel took Damon's proffered bill and slapped his change on the counter. "Need a bag?"

"Hey, why bother, Mel?" Damon said, winking at Mel's daughter. "I'll just drink it in the parking lot." As Damon turned to leave, he caught sight of Thea and stopped. Touching the brim of his black cap, he said, "Hey, Prebble, care to join me in a cold one?"

"Damon," she whispered urgently, "what's going on here? Why does this man treat you that way? He's… he's…You're his customer!"

As Damon looked at her, the biting sarcasm faded a little from his expression. "True," he said. "But not his favorite."

Mel began ringing up Thea's purchases without saying a word to her.

"I can't imagine why you shop here," Thea exclaimed, her voice louder than she meant it to be. "You don't have to tolerate such treatment. It's degrading."

Mel didn't raise his gaze from her cart, though he obviously overheard. "If you don't like it, lady, there's another market down the street." He hit the total button on the cash register. "Seventy-four eighty-five."

Thea regarded him coldly. "Seventy-four eighty-five? That sounds like too much to me for what I'm receiving."

"Too much?" Mel bellowed. "Do you want to see the tape?"

Thea blushed hotly at the sound of his booming voice echoing around the store. "That won't be necessary," she said primly. "I shall take your advice and ask Mr. Free to show me the market down the street." She tapped the counter with her polished nail. "Seventy-four eighty-five may not be the largest total you ring up today, but it's a great deal too much for me to give to a merchant who treats me and...my friends in this ignominious manner."

With that, Thea spun on her heel and headed for the door. She caught sight of Damon from the corner of her eye as she strode by him. From his slack jaw and rounded eyes, she had the impression he was in shock.

"Igno...igno...whatever!" Mel roared. "What about these groceries?"

Thea turned from the door to give Mel her haughtiest stare. "You'll just have to reshelve them. I don't feel welcome enough in your store to remain for the time it would take to do it myself."

Damon held the door for her then followed her outside. "Unbelievable, Prebble!" he said, his tone—though thick with laughter—for once devoid of sarcasm. "I'd never have guessed you had it in you." He traced a finger along her spine. "What do you know…a backbone. I'm impressed."

Thea spun around and poked him in the chest. "If you knew that man would start a fight like that, why did you go in there? You behaved like…an adolescent!"

"Won't deny it," Damon said. He ran his gaze appreciatively over some women entering the store. "You wouldn't be thinking about giving me one of those boring lectures on the subject, would you?" He flashed her one of his heart-stopping grins. "If so, I just remembered another appointment."

Thea glowered at him, trying to resist his engaging grin. She told herself he turned it on and off like a faucet, just like her French stepfather, René. Worse, she could still feel the imprint of Damon's fingers running down her back.

But her confrontation with Mel—exactly the sort of public display Chelsea had always taught her to shun—had left her shaky, her emotional defenses breached. Now she was melting from one look at the wonderful long dimples that framed Damon's mouth, at the sun crinkles beside his dark eyes. Giving herself a mental shake, Thea walked to her car.

"The other store's right down the street," Damon told her, pointing down Main Street. "They'll be glad to see you. They always wanted Dora's business."

"What was that really all about, Damon?" Thea asked as she stepped into her car.

"It goes back a long time," Damon said, the stony expression returning to his face. "I'm sorry you got in the middle of it. Though I admit, it was a kick watching you in action."

"Well, Mel's going to be sorry, too," Thea said. "I plan to move my business to the other store permanently. And when I get this B&B up and running, my account will be large enough to notice."

She pulled on the door, but Damon held it open. "*If* would be a better word, Prebble. You don't have the variance yet." His charcoal eyes met hers but revealed nothing. "And the smart money would be on your not getting it."

"I don't know why you're so sure," Thea said. "I took my request to the Town Hall this morning. The city council meets two weeks from Tuesday, and the clerk was sure I'd hear right after that."

"Yeah," Damon said. "Maybe even before." He shut her door.

Thea watched him saunter toward his motorcycle. As he approached it, Roni emerged from the store, arms laden with a customer's groceries. He leaned on the saddle of his bike, waiting while she put them in the customer's car. The smile he gave her when she joined him looked so genuine and warm, Thea felt a stab of...

Not jealousy. She didn't feel *that* way about Damon Free. But maybe a little envy. Damon had never directed a full-fledged smile like that at her. Sardonic laughter and the rare quick grin were all he'd ever bestowed on Thea—the minimum he must feel he owed Dora. As Thea looked at him chatting with Roni, their hands resting side by side on the handlebars, she realized she wanted more.

All her reason shouted at her to stop such foolishness, but another part of her—the wild Prebble part?—wanted Damon to look at her the way he was looking at this woman. As though he was truly glad to see her, as though—

As though what?

Thea brought herself up short. What on earth was she thinking? She turned the key in the ignition and gunned the engine.

As she shifted into reverse, a petite, sparkly-eyed blonde joined Roni and Damon by his motorcycle. Letting her fingers rest on Damon's biceps, she gazed intently into his eyes while she spoke to him. Without breaking contact with the blonde, Damon leaned forward to give Roni a kiss.

Oh, good Lord, Thea thought, *what will they let him get away with? Don't they have any pride?*

When Thea drove out of the lot, the blonde was cuddling up behind Damon on the seat of his motorcycle.

The next day shortly after noon, Damon walked through Thea's front door after the most perfunctory knock. She looked down at him from the landing, where she was trying to peel off old wallpaper without destroying the plaster underneath.

"If you used a steamer for that," Damon said, "it'd save you a lot of swearing and frustration."

"Damon," Thea said, "do you call that a knock?"

"I haven't knocked here since I was thirteen," he said. "Besides, I'm here doing you a favor." He held up an envelope and a key, and Thea started down the stairs toward him. "That's the key to Dora's post office box. Silas gave it to me when I agreed to be caretaker. You need to get the box transferred to your name."

Thea nodded. "Will you take a cut in pay when I start picking up the mail?"

"Pay?" Damon asked in a cold tone, his lips curving into a sneer.

Thea's cheeks warmed. "Silas told me—"

"Don't believe everything you hear, Prebble," Damon said. "Especially about me."

Thea looked hard at Damon, wishing she could see inside him. Silas thought Damon didn't understand friendship, but maybe it was Silas who didn't understand. Apparently, Damon had watched Dora's house, picked up her mail, even cleaned up her bedroom just because he'd been so fond of her. Maybe Silas didn't know Damon planned to refuse pay for his services. More likely he didn't realize how much Dora had meant to Damon.

Thea wondered if those women Damon seemed to collect got to see this softer side of him all the time. Dora must have. Why did he hide it from Thea? All she got were these occasional flashes of insight into his true nature.

Most of the time, he kept his supercool facade firmly in place. But this time when he returned her look with all the warmth of a thick stone wall, Thea didn't believe it. Under that aloof exterior beat a soft heart full of intense emotions. She was sure of it.

He held out the envelope. "I guess the variance committee thought—"

Thea snatched the letter. "My answer already?" she cried. "I told you they wouldn't have any problem with it."

"You can tell that through the envelope?" Damon asked.

"Why else would they answer so quickly?" Thea said, going to the kitchen for a knife. "Undoubtedly they had no problems with it and just approved it without a meeting."

When she unfolded the letter, Thea's jaw dropped. The committee hadn't even bothered to write a response—they'd simply returned *her* letter with DENIED written across it in large red letters.

She looked up at Damon, stunned. Her hands began to shake. "How...how could..."

Damon took the letter from her fingers and glanced at it. His frown grew deep and angry, but he said nothing. He pulled a chair out from the kitchen table and pushed Thea into it. "Want a beer or something?"

Thea gave him a withering look. "Oh, that would help a lot, Damon."

"Always does," Damon said, pulling open the fridge.

"'Cept you don't seem to have any cold." He turned back to her. "How about a—"

"Damon, I don't need alcohol!"

"Yeah? What do you need, then?" He flicked up a brow, giving her a suggestive grin. "Besides—"

"Answers." She pointed at the chair on the other side of the table. "Please, tell me what's going on. Why did this happen? You *knew* it would happen. Talk to me."

Damon stared out the kitchen window. From behind, he looked relaxed. But his fists on the counter, the knuckles white from the strength of his grip, gave him away.

"Damon, you know I've already invested over a hundred and fifty thousand dollars in this house," she said, trying to keep her tone neutral. "What you don't know is how much of my...soul I've invested in it, too." She crossed the kitchen and pushed her recipe box along the counter till he couldn't help seeing it. "Look in there. I've collected those since I was thirteen."

Damon lifted the lid and glanced inside. He pulled out a few recipe cards, then a pattern for a prairie dress, a stenciling outline. He turned to look at her.

"Okay, Prebble," he said, "I'm impressed." He put everything back in her box, careful to return each item to the right spot. "I'm beginning to see why Dora believed in you."

Thea reached over and slammed the box lid, barely missing Damon's fingers. "Damon!" she said. "What's going on?"

Damon pretended to count his fingers as if to make sure Thea hadn't chopped one off. But when he let his gaze meet hers, she was startled at the rage she saw there. She blinked in surprise, and Damon quickly hid his anger under his mask of indifference.

"It's simple, Prebble," he said. "Mel—your friendly grocer—is chairman of the variance committee."

"Oh, no," Thea groaned. "Why didn't you warn me before I infuriated him?"

"I didn't have much chance," Damon said. "But it wouldn't have mattered anyway. He wrote you off way before you insulted him to his face. Most likely as soon as you rode to Silas's office with me. Your only hope was to fire me as caretaker on the spot."

"That makes no sense whatsoever," Thea said. "What should I have done? Insist you mess up the rooms you'd tidied? Break a few windows and steal something valuable to prove you hadn't been watching over the place?"

Damon lifted one shoulder in a shrug. Every movement he made seemed tight. "If you'd called Silas and had me thrown off the property for good, that'd probably have satisfied him."

"And how would *that* have helped?" Thea asked. "Does Mel have a tap on Silas's phone?"

Damon gave a short bark of a laugh. "You've never lived in a little town before, have you?"

"No," Thea said dejectedly, "and I'm beginning to wonder if I know how." She sighed. "I guess I should have asked more questions before I quit my job and drove two thousand miles."

Stepping to the refrigerator, she pulled out iced tea. Without asking Damon, she poured two glasses and handed him one. Then she sat back at the table, folding her hands in her lap.

"Okay," she said, forcing a businesslike tone. "Here's one. Why does Mel hate you so much?"

Damon shook his head. "It's a long story, fifteen years long. And boring." He took a swallow of the tea. "And none of your business. Besides, it may be a little more personal between Mel and me than with the rest of the town—but not much."

Thea pursed her lips. "I suppose Dora knew?"

"You're not Dora," Damon said, putting his empty glass on the counter. "Not to me or Mel. Truth is, Mel'd never have gotten the committee to deny this request if Dora'd made it. Whole town loved her."

Thea closed her eyes a second. She couldn't let herself think about Dora now. "Do you honestly believe Mel would let his personal feelings influence his decision on...?" The anger in Damon's face made the words quit in her throat.

"How can you doubt it?" He picked up the letter and waved it at her. "Do you need to look at this again?"

Anger and dismay struggled for control of Thea's emotions, but she fought them down. "Well, he's not going to get away with it." Very carefully, she picked up her glass and took a sip, then returned it to the table. "This is business, my *livelihood*." Her words, the realization behind them, shattered her forced calm. "How *dare* that man use his position for some kind of personal revenge? It's a vendetta. It's outrageous! It's the most blatant misuse of power I've ever heard of."

Damon smiled sardonically. "You must not have heard of many."

"Enough," she grumbled. Too angry to remain still, she paced the kitchen, slapping the counter when she came close enough. "Well, he has met his match. He's not going to get away with this, Damon. I'll appeal it."

"Yeah?" Damon leaned back against the counter to get out of her way. "Who to?"

"The city council to start with," Thea said. "They're the ones who actually make this decision and they don't meet for two more weeks. They can't even have looked at it."

"You don't have a chance," Damon said. "They'll rubber-stamp the committee. They always do."

"They won't this time," Thea said grimly. "Not without

hearing from me." She poked a finger in Damon's direction. "And they'll make the decision in front of a lot of reporters, trust me on that. They'll look darn foolish if they go ahead with this decision, and everyone in the state will know about it."

Damon looked slightly stunned at her vehemence. "It won't be that hard, Thea. What did you say to them in your letter?"

"Just what you'd told me, you know, all the stuff you planned to do to restore the house."

"You specifically stated I would do the work?"

"Of course. I said I had hired you."

"No wonder," Damon groaned. "Just tell them you've changed your mind...decided to hire a different contractor. Tell 'em you fired me because you heard I was so unreliable. You'll get your variance next Tuesday."

"I will do no such thing!" Thea was shocked to hear the rage in her voice. "*You're* what this fight is about, Damon." She waved a hand in his general direction. "It's time this town gave you a chance. Look at the way you cared for Dora, have taken care of her property since she died. You have a heart, Damon, and you have ethics. I trust you implicitly to fix up this house."

The words were out of Thea's mouth before she knew she planned to say them. But the moment she heard them, she knew they were true. She believed Damon could fix the house, because he had told *Auntie* he would. Damon did his best to hide most of his feelings from Thea, but he had not been able to disguise the way he felt about Dora. He would never have promised her he would restore her house unless he knew he could.

But Damon was looking at her now as if she'd grown two heads. "*You* trust *me* implicitly?"

Something in his tone made Thea even more sure she was right. "I certainly do, at least in this regard." She smiled. "It's unfair for the town to judge you incapable of an honest day's work when they won't give you a chance to prove what you can do." She pounded a fist on the counter. "They'll see."

"Thea," he said, his tone slightly awed, even more suspicious, "what's going on? You fight Mel in his store over some alleged insult to me, now you want to take on the whole city council." He cocked his head. "You turn into St. George or something?" He gave her one of his slow grins which very nearly distracted her.

Damon kept his words light, his smile tempting, but something in his voice touched Thea and made her heart beat oddly. She had the strongest feeling he was serious, very, very serious.

"If I don't fight your dragon now, Damon, I'll lose my business before it's even begun." Her voice began to shake as she spoke, and she realized how much such a loss would mean to her as well as Damon. "I'll lose my whole reason for coming west, my independence, my freedom."

"Exactly," Damon said, his eyes still locked on hers. "That's your battle. You don't need to take mine on."

Thea plopped her hands on her hips. "Mel made it *my* battle. I won't let him, or the rest of the town, do this to you, Damon. I won't let them do it to me. They're going to find out I can hire whomever I please."

The odd look Damon was giving her—as if he'd never seen her before in his life—made her wonder if anyone had ever fought for him before. Well, if not, it was time someone did.

"This is an injustice, Damon."

"There's a lot of injustice in the world."

"Well, I was brought up to fight it," she declared.

"That was your daddy doing the fighting," Damon said. "It was his job."

"Well *I* believed in what he was doing," Thea said. "In

what he taught me and the way he stood up for me. And *we* are going to fight this. All the way to the Supreme Court if we have to."

Damon's brows rose dramatically. "We?"

Thea blushed. "Me."

Damon caught her shoulders as she was about to spin away again. She looked up at his dark eyes. Her stomach fluttered at the intensity she saw there. "You've always been…such a wimp." He continued to hold her shoulders. "Hiding behind your daddy and all those rules, never taking a single step someone didn't show you how to take."

Thea was startled at the disrespect in Damon's voice. Obviously, despite the little kindnesses he'd begun to show her, his opinion of her hadn't changed much. Or was he testing her, checking to see if he could trust her or not? That made her stop and think a moment about what she was getting into.

Damon snorted and dropped his hands. "That's what I figured."

"You figured wrong," she said. "I was just remembering Dora. I never got to see as much of her as I wanted because I was doing just what you said—following all those dictates of all those other people. That will not happen to me again."

"Yeah?"

Thea tapped his chest. "Before this day is out, Damon, the city council will have me on its agenda for the next meeting."

Damon gave her a long look, emotions warring on his face, a muscle twitching in his cheek. "You'll regret this," Damon said. "But I guess I can't stop you." He left the kitchen, muttering, "Probably won't regret it half as much as I will."

Thea followed him down the hall. "I don't suppose you

want to give me just a hint of what they have against you?" she said as he reached for the screen-door handle.

Damon chuckled, turning such a suggestive grin on her, she almost backed away from him. "Sure, Prebble, I'll give you a hint."

He grabbed her shoulders and pulled her tight to him. His right hand slid to her backside, massaging gently as he pulled her into the vee of his legs.

This time, Thea didn't even pretend to resist; she knew it was useless. She found herself pressing closer to Damon, trying to bring more of her body into contact with him.

His head dipped toward hers. She couldn't take her eyes from his lips, full and soft, yet determined. So determined.

Hers fluttered open, ready to…to protest?…to welcome him? He touched his mouth to her cheek, nibbled along her jawbone to her earlobe, his hot breath swirling against the whorls of her ear, making her quiver.

"Like this hint, Prebble?" he whispered huskily. "This is all the town thinks I'm good for. Mel particularly." His lips returned to hers, teasing them with his tongue. "What about you? Do *you* think I'm good for anything else?"

He lowered her to the bench of the hall tree. Before she could make sense of his words, the door shut behind him.

CHAPTER SIX

THEA didn't know how long she sat on the bench in the hall, waiting for her desire to quiet. But it wouldn't. For years she had lied to herself. It was time to face the truth.

Damon Free had disturbed her since she was a young girl taking her first steps into womanhood. Damon had recognized the changes she was making before anyone else. He teased her about it, enough to scare her a little. But she didn't want him to stop. He made her feel...womanly, older...pretty.

Had that been what Father really heard on the phone back then? Not that this boy had a police record, but Thea's first fluttering female interest in a boy? So new she hadn't recognized it herself.

On her next visit to Pine Butte, she recognized it. But by then she knew to fear it, to avoid it—at least with a man like Damon. Yet he'd kissed her anyway, despite her honest wish to abstain from any such contact.

That kiss! How it had tormented her through college and graduate school. At first, she'd told herself that her dates were simply too young to kiss like Damon. But as the years passed and her dates changed from boys to men, the harder it became to believe that.

The men she went out with now, including J.P., were as old as Damon or older. Their experience...well, who knew if their experience was as vast as Damon's in *that* way. Pleasing women of one sort or another did seem to be Damon's long suit.

Thea sighed and gave up. She couldn't rationalize this away. Damon Free stirred her, brought out every Prebble characteristic she had been taught to abhor. Worse, she enjoyed it.

She even enjoyed his company. This afternoon in the kitchen, when the chip had slipped just a bit from his shoulder, Thea had wanted him to stay longer. Even before he kissed her senseless in the hallway, she had wanted him to stay and talk.

Had he softened toward her? She thought so, a little, though she couldn't exactly put her finger on it. Maybe they simply had a common enemy now, and that was bringing them closer. Maybe it wasn't the Prebble flaw at all.

Oh, who was she kidding?

It was the next morning before Thea's emotions had quieted enough for her to discuss the business license and all its ramifications calmly. She missed Silas at his office but tracked him down at the Doubletree Café where, his secretary assured Thea, he conducted half his business. She joined him at the table, turning down steak and eggs but accepting coffee.

After the waitress had brought her a fresh cup, Thea explained what she'd done thus far to get her variance and the result.

"I'm going to appeal it, Silas," Thea said. "It's really the city council that gets to decide this. I'll prepare—"

"You won't have trouble with that," Silas interrupted. "Simply hire a contractor of repute."

"I have a contractor," Thea said coldly.

"Few would agree with you, my dear." Silas looked more disapproving than worried. "I hope you haven't let him bamboozle you, too, as he did your aunt."

"No indeed," Thea said. "But I won't let one prejudiced grocer—"

"Mel has his reasons," Silas said. "Good ones."

"I'm sure he thinks so," Thea said, "but I doubt I'd agree with him."

Silas sat silent a moment, studying the fake wood grain in the Formica-topped table. Thea almost hoped he'd again refuse to tell her anything, as he had the morning of the will reading. It wasn't that she didn't want to know what this was all about; she just wished she could hear it—whatever it was—from someone besides Silas. Someone who knew Damon's good side.

"I dislike repeating gossip," Silas said with distaste, "but I feel compelled. I cannot leave you...unprotected with that man."

"Oh, honestly," Thea said, exasperated. "You make him sound like a disease."

"Close." Silas looked so pompous, Thea wondered if he practiced the look in a mirror. "Mel has a very beautiful daughter, Roni. She was every boy's dream in high school. Mel, wisely, wouldn't let her go out with Damon. Even Damon's father advised Mel to keep Roni away from his son."

His *father*? A rush of sadness washed over Thea. What sort of man would treat his own son that way? Her father might be demanding, sometimes even oppressively so, but he was always on her side.

"Mel learned later that Damon connived his way into Roni's good graces by helping her with math homework. It wasn't something anyone would expect, since he never handed in any homework himself." Silas quit eating and pushed his plate away. "Of course, it was simply a devious stratagem on his part."

"I can't imagine any harm coming to a girl, even a beautiful girl," Thea said acidly, "over math homework."

"Hmmph!" Silas declared. "But it didn't end there. Roni sneaked out on dates with him that no doubt he insisted be part of his 'pay' for helping her with math."

"I don't believe that, Silas," Thea said. "You know he won't accept pay for being caretaker, either. I think you misjudge—"

"My dear," Silas interrupted, "you have been in town a few days. Don't try to tell me about Damon Free. He ruined that young woman's life, got her pregnant and wouldn't marry her. She had been accepted at Georgetown University, where she planned to study medicine. Instead she's a grocer." He paused for effect. "And a single mother. The boy is nine years old."

Thea couldn't answer. For all his pompousness, Silas was right. She didn't know Damon. If he'd do that to a woman, she didn't know him at all.

"He...does he..." Thea looked down and saw she had shredded her paper napkin. She longed to press her water glass to her flaming cheeks, but she couldn't make such a revealing gesture in front of Silas. "Does he claim the boy? Take him for weekends?"

Silas snorted. "Damon gives little Matt rides on the motorcycle. That's his idea of paternity."

Thea had an overwhelming urge to flee the café...and Pine Butte. Get in her fast car and forget she'd ever met Damon Free. As if that was possible.

Fortunately, Silas brought her back to earth. "So you can see what you're up against, trying to persuade the variance committee Damon Free deserves even to live in Pine Butte, much less to be hired for such a serious historical project."

"That's pretty strong, Silas," Thea said. "Running people out of town for that kind of thing went out with Queen Victoria."

"Society's been going downhill ever since." Silas harrumphed.

The waitress refilled their cups, giving Thea a moment to regain her composure. "If the town has such a low opinion of Damon," she asked, "why is he still here? Why doesn't he go somewhere else and start over?"

"He did for a while." Silas sounded uncomfortable at last. "Of course, I didn't discuss his reasons for coming back with *him*. But your aunt told me he came home for her. She had done a great deal for him in his youth, and he came home to take care of her in her declining years. Or so she said."

Thea's head spun. How could Silas know something like that about Damon, something probably few people knew, and still judge him as harshly as he did? Damon had so many sides, yet he seemed to show only one to the townspeople.

"And his son?" she asked. "Do you think that had anything to do with his coming back?"

Silas made a noise of refined disgust. "My dear Thea, please do not let that devil hoodwink you the way he did your aunt. The way he does all those other young women. You don't want to end up like Roni. And who knows how many others."

"Others?" Thea squeaked. "What makes you think there are others?"

"Because I am not as naive as you young women appear to be." Silas let out a pained sigh. "I would never forgive myself if I let my dear friend's niece, for whom I feel somewhat responsible, fall under that man's spell." He put his damp palm over her hand. "My dear, don't let your hormones make this decision for you."

Thea snatched her hand back. "Silas, don't be ridiculous!"

Inside she was squirming. If Silas could see it, it must be obvious to everyone that she desired Damon. She might as well tattoo "Prebble flaw" across her brow.

Silas had the grace to look uncomfortable.

"Just get me on the city council agenda for its next meeting."

He picked up the check. "I'm sorry I can't dissuade you. I hope you don't regret your actions."

Thea remained at the table after Silas left, staring at her cold coffee. Just yesterday, Damon had warned her not to believe everything she heard, especially about him. Could he have added, especially not from Silas? After all, Silas was the one who'd told her Damon was taking pay to be caretaker.

But would Silas make up something like this? A son?

She thought of the times she'd seen Roni and Damon together and wondered why Damon *hadn't* wanted to marry her. He apparently suffered Mel's insults in the store just to see her. Thea shook her head. She wouldn't make up her mind about this until she talked to Damon.

Talk to Damon? How was she going to do that? Did one get to quiz one's contractor about his previous affairs? Somehow that didn't sound like the sort of qualification that seemed applicable to installing canvas siding.

Thea sighed. She had to be honest with herself. She wanted to know whether Silas's story was true because the thought of Damon holding that beautiful woman, making love to her, sharing a child with her, filled Thea with a painful twist of emotions that she refused to call jealousy.

Why would she be jealous? Jealous of an affair he had years ago? No, this was more like...more like... Thea bit her lip. This was exactly like jealousy.

She couldn't help herself. She wondered what it would be like to have Damon desire her that way, to want more than the disturbing kisses he'd given her in the hall. How would it feel to have him take her to his bed, to make love to her all night long, to wake up next to him in the morning? Even more, she wanted to know how it would feel to have Damon's face light up when he saw her, the way it did when he saw Roni.

She wondered if her face lit up so obviously when she saw Damon. She couldn't say exactly when she had quit dreading his visits. Had she ever truly done so? Yes, surely she had at first.

Oh, the man was driving her crazy!

Thea's phone was ringing when she walked through her front door. "Theadora," Norman said when she picked up the receiver, "I just had a very disturbing call from your lawyer."

Thea groaned. She wanted to strangle Silas. "He's not my lawyer, Father. He's lawyer to the estate."

"He thinks he's your lawyer."

"If that were true," Thea said, her voice as acid as it ever got with her father, "I could fire him and sue him for malpractice. Isn't everything one says to a lawyer confidential?"

"I always thought so," Norman said dryly.

"And what did Silas tell you? Everything I've said to him since I arrived in Pine Butte? Did he have any scruples about any single thing?"

Norman hesitated. "No, Theadora, I don't believe he did." He cleared his throat. "But you can't think he's out of line when you're about to—"

"Yes, Father, I do." Thea gathered her courage. "*I* am about to make a decision about *my* inheritance," she said. "In fact, I've already made it."

A longer pause ensued this time. "You're twenty-four. I can only advise you, not order you around. But from what Silas told me, I'm afraid you may be making a serious mistake in your choice of builder."

"I'm not," Thea said firmly. "I know more about the whole picture than Silas, no matter what he told you."

"Very well," Norman said, using his crisp command

tone. "You are a Birch. I expect you to use good judgment."

Thea swallowed. *Father* trusted her judgment? Had he forgotten the Prebble wild streak? He must truly believe he'd trained it out of her. Well, that wasn't so surprising; till a week ago, she'd thought so herself.

"Of course, Father."

"When the restoration's nearly complete, I'll fly out with J.P. and we'll see about the sale."

"But Father, I—"

As usual, Norman hung up without saying goodbye.

Thea hung up the phone and looked around the kitchen, trying to think of a chore, any chore, more pressing than cleaning out those upstairs rooms. She hadn't heard any scurrying mouse noises since she brought the cats home. She hoped they'd finished the job of evicting the mice. After all, wouldn't any mouse with a modicum of instinct move out at the first smell of cat?

Grabbing the broom, she climbed the stairs resolutely. At the door to Dora's room, she saw the kitties curled up together on the chaise in a puddle of sunlight. Their soft black fur seemed to beg for stroking.

As Thea passed Dora's bed, the edge of her vision caught something out of place on the faded old quilt. Something...wrong. She turned to look.

"Oh, *ii-ick!*" she shrieked. "Ugh, ugh." Turning, she fled from the room.

Leaning against the wall, she closed her eyes, which was a mistake. Her mind pictured just as clearly that disemboweled mouse corpse disgustingly displayed on Dora's pillow. How on *earth* was she going get rid of...gag...it?

Thea suddenly decided this might be the time to take the walk down to the lake she'd been promising herself. That she knew Damon sometimes worked at a building site there surely had nothing to do with her decision.

Outside, she noticed a few storm clouds gathering as she picked her way down the steep hill toward the lake. The path she had taken daily as a child was overgrown and barely noticeable. Obviously, Dora hadn't done much swimming the past few years.

At the shore, she saw that, despite the houses that had been constructed in small clusters around the lake, the vast majority of the land was still undeveloped. Windsurfers sailed by each other near the public beach a mile to the east, but most of the wide blue lake was empty.

A half mile or more to the west, three houses were under construction. Thea took off her sandals to shake out the dirt and pebbles. Hidden behind the dunes, a barbed-wire fence that hadn't been there when she was a girl separated her shoreline from her neighbors. Dora must have had it built when the ranches next to her land subdivided.

Thea climbed through the wires, catching her new jeans on one of the barbs. She eyed the small hole. Better than a hole in her flesh, she thought philosophically, continuing toward the houses. Her feet hurt by the time she got close enough to see that the house with a motorcycle parked outside was, of course, the farthest away.

Nearing it, she felt silly. Maybe Damon was right calling her a wimp. She'd walked over a mile, tearing her jeans and blistering her feet, just to get someone to take a dead mouse off her bed. Someone who—if he was there as she hoped—was earning money he no doubt needed. Perhaps she should—

"Thea?" a vaguely familiar voice said. "Aren't you Thea Birch, Dora's niece?"

"Yes," she said, looking up toward the stepless doorway several feet above her. Damon's friend, Jerry, stood in the entry holding out a hand to help her up. "I'm looking for Damon. Is he here?"

"Not now." He grabbed her wrist and pulled her up.

"He oughta be back in a couple of hours. Something wrong?"

"Not exactly," Thea said.

She wondered if Damon's boss knew how irregularly he showed up for work. Even more, she wondered if he'd continue to keep such a schedule when he went to work for her. Her house would take years to complete!

Jerry must have misinterpreted her worried frown. "You need to phone him?"

"No, it's not that serious," Thea said hurriedly. "It's just...I found a mouse. Well, actually, the cats found a mouse."

Jerry started laughing. Not that she blamed him.

"They left it right on my bed."

"Dead and gory?"

"Disgusting."

Jerry shook his head, still chuckling. "It can't hurt you dead."

"It can, actually," Thea said. "It can make me ill."

"You want me to come up and throw it away?" he asked, nodding up the hill. "That's quite a walk just to get rid of a mouse. Did it drive you out of the house?"

"I can stay in the house," Thea said. "But I doubt I can go in my bedroom. I thought maybe Damon could just stop by after work." She gave him an embarrassed smile. "At least then I won't have to sleep on the couch."

Jerry couldn't stop smiling. "I'm sure he won't mind. It's not that far out of his way." He picked up a thermos. "Want some coffee?"

"No, thank you," Thea said. "I'm too hot for coffee." Jerry seemed much nicer to her here than he had on Main Street. "What I'd really like is an ice-cold white wine spritzer, but I don't suppose you have one of those?"

"Oh, sure. Have 'em all the time." Jerry's sarcasm

PLAY
HARLEQUIN'S

LUCKY HEARTS
GAME

AND YOU GET

★ **FREE BOOKS**

★ **A FREE GIFT**

★ **AND MUCH MORE**

TURN THE PAGE AND
DEAL YOURSELF IN

PLAY "LUCKY HEARTS" AND YOU GET . . .

★ **Exciting Harlequin romance novels—FREE**

★ **PLUS a Lovely Simulated Pearl Drop Necklace—FREE**

THEN CONTINUE YOUR LUCKY STREAK WITH A SWEETHEART OF A DEAL

1. Play Lucky Hearts as instructed on the opposite page.
2. Send back this card and you'll receive brand-new Harlequin Romance® novels. These books have a cover price of $3.25 each, but they are yours to keep absolutely free.
3. There's no catch. You're under no obligation to buy anything. We charge nothing — ZERO — for your first shipment. And you don't have to make any minimum number of purchases — not even one!
4. The fact is thousands of readers enjoy receiving books by mail from the Harlequin Reader Service®. They like the convenience of home delivery…they like getting the best new novels BEFORE they're available in stores…and they love our discount prices!
5. We hope that after receiving your free books you'll want to remain a subscriber. But the choice is yours — to continue or cancel, anytime at all! So why not take us up on our invitation, with no risk of any kind. You'll be glad you did!

HARLEQUIN'S

With a coin—scratch off the silver card and check below to see what we have for you.

YES! I have scratched off the silver card. Please send me all the free books and gift for which I qualify. I understand that I am under no obligation to purchase any books, as explained on the back and on the opposite page.

116 CIH CARL (U-H-R-08/97)

NAME

ADDRESS   APT.

CITY   STATE   ZIP

Twenty-one gets you 4 free books, and a free simulated pearl drop necklace

Twenty gets you 4 free books

Nineteen gets you 3 free books

Eighteen gets you 2 free books

THE HARLEQUIN READER SERVICE®: HERE'S HOW IT WORKS

Accepting free books places you under no obligation to buy anything. You may keep the books and gift and return the shipping statement marked "cancel". If you do not cancel, about a month later we'll send you 6 additional novels, and bill you just $2.67 each plus 25¢ delivery per book and applicable sales tax, if any.* That's the complete price–and compared to cover prices of $3.25 each–quite a bargain! You may cancel at any time, but if you choose to continue, every month we'll send you 6 more books, which you may either purchase at the discount price…or return to us and cancel your subscription.

*Terms and prices subject to change without notice. Sales tax applicable in N.Y.

wasn't as biting as Damon's, but it was just as obvious. "Keep Perrier in the cooler just in case."

Thea smiled at his weak humor. "Well, I'd better let you get back to work. You probably have some sort of schedule you need to stick to, don't you?" She winced, knowing she was being as subtle as a heart attack. But she couldn't stop herself. "Or can you guys just...sort of...take all the time you want on this house?"

Jerry regarded her a moment. "If you mean Damon, why don't you say so?"

Thea's cheeks warmed under his scrutiny. "You know he's agreed to do the restoration on my aunt's house?"

Jerry gave a short laugh. "'Agreed' ain't exactly the way he described it."

"But he did. He—"

"I know," Jerry said. "You got him in the scruples. Most people don't know he has any." He shrugged. "What the hell, I thought he oughta do it anyway."

"You did?" Thea said, surprised. "Why?"

"It's one summer," Jerry said, making a throwaway gesture with his hands. "If he didn't do it, it'd bother him the rest of his life."

"Why on earth should it?" Thea asked.

"'Cause he'd always remember that he didn't do the last thing Dora asked him to do. She was a great old lady, you know? We all liked her."

"I did, too," Thea said sadly. "But I understand Damon did a great deal for Dora when she was alive. I can't believe he owes her anything more. I hope he doesn't later regret agreeing to this."

"He'll work it out." Jerry put on a pair of wire-rimmed glasses. "Says you're gonna do some of the work."

"Yes, I agreed to that," Thea said. "How could I not?"

"Good luck," Jerry told her. "He's a perfectionist, demanding as hell."

Puzzled, Thea frowned in confusion. If Damon was such a perfectionist, why wasn't *he* here working, instead of letting Jerry do it all? She kicked some sawdust and wood pieces out of the way as she followed him back to the table saw where he was working.

"Jerry?" she said, raising her voice as he flicked on the saw.

"Yeah?" He picked up a two-by-six from a stack of boards.

"Damon, um..." She nearly had to shout to be heard over the whine of the saw. Giving up discretion, she decided on directness. "His work habits don't exactly inspire confidence in a prospective employer."

Jerry turned, his expression disdainful. "There's something you ought to know about Damon before you go shooting off your mouth."

Thea tensed, dreading what she was about to learn about Damon now. "Yes?"

Jerry flicked off the saw.

"Yeah, Jer." In the sudden silence, Damon's voice echoed around the huge, empty house. "What's that?"

Jerry gave Damon a look Thea would not have described as submissive. But after a few seconds' clash of their eyes, Damon obviously won.

"Ah, hell," Jerry said. "I guess you can tell her yourself."

"Right," Damon said. "I can."

Thea let her own gaze meet Damon's, surprised at the defiance she read there. She wondered what bit of knowledge Jerry had been about to tell her. It must have been very personal to annoy Damon this much.

And what could be more personal than an affair that resulted in a child out of wedlock? For some reason, Thea couldn't face the prospect of hearing Damon tell her about fathering a baby.

"Don't worry, Damon," she said. "I've already heard."

Damon flicked up a brow. "That right?"

She returned his ironic gaze. "And it did nothing to influence my choice of you as my contractor."

Surprisingly—at least it surprised Thea—she was having no trouble meeting Damon's eyes and talking about this. For that matter, she was having the same pleasant, slightly excited, reaction to seeing him that she had *before* she knew he had fathered a son. Chelsea would faint at such behavior.

Thea changed the subject. "I, um, came down here looking for you."

"Checking my work before you let me start on your house?" His annoyance turned to sarcasm.

Though she hadn't come for that reason, she couldn't deny it, not after quizzing Jerry about Damon's work habits. She squirmed under Damon's cold look.

Ignoring tension so thick his saw could have cut it, Jerry grinned. "She's got a much bigger problem than that. Been a murder up at her house."

"What?"

"Oh, honestly!" Thea jammed her hands on her hips. "My kittens killed something—a mouse, I assume—but I didn't look closely enough to be certain. I don't know if I would have been able to tell..." She stopped, her words catching in her suddenly gagging throat. She moved a fist to her mouth.

Damon began laughing, his irritation seemingly dissipated. "Maybe they're not so useless after all. Where'd they leave it, right on your bed?"

"Yes!" Thea said. "I can't sleep there." She lifted a sandaled foot toward him. "I couldn't even go back in to get shoes." In the face of his hilarity, she grew a little irritated herself. "I certainly don't expect you to take *more* time off just for me, Mr. Free. I just thought perhaps you could stop by at the end of your workday—whenever that is."

Damon shook his head. "Hard to believe I almost quit thinking you were a wimp."

Despite his words, Thea felt her shoulders relax at his teasing. Something sounded different about the way he said "wimp" today. His tone just didn't seem to carry the sting it had twenty-four hours ago.

"I guess you save your courage for battling windmills, not dead mice on your bed."

"It's not just dead," Thea exclaimed. "It's beheaded or disemboweled. It's thoroughly disgusting."

"That's why you wash your hands after you pick it up and throw it out," Damon said in a reasonable tone, as if he was making a real suggestion.

Thea simply shuddered.

"Prissy."

"I am *not* prissy," Thea insisted primly. "Just a little squeamish."

"Ri-ight," Damon and Jerry said in unison.

"C'mon," Damon said, "I'll give you a ride home. You'll wreck your feet walking back up the hill in those."

"Sandals won't do her much good on your bike," Jerry said.

"I've still got Darlene's boots," Damon said, eyeing Thea's feet.

"Your bike?" Thea said nervously, wondering if Darlene was the sparkly-eyed blonde or some other woman she had yet to meet. "You mean your motorcycle?"

As Jerry began running the saw again, Damon took Thea's arm and led her across the scattered subfloor to an opening that one day might turn into a door. He jumped to the ground, then turned to lift her down by the waist. With her eyes glued to the sight of his huge motorcycle, she barely noticed the sensation.

She could easily tell the bikes apart now: Jerry's suddenly looked much smaller, and safer. Surely it couldn't go as fast as Damon's; probably it wouldn't make as much noise. And it had a curved bar behind the passenger seat that would keep her from sliding off the back end. Damon's didn't have one of those.

Damon lifted the lid on a little trunk behind his seat and pulled out a pair of leather boots. "Put these on," he said. "You want a helmet?"

"Aren't we just going up the hill?"

Damon nodded. "We'll ride out to the highway on this road around the lake—" he pointed at a long, curving gravel road that disappeared around a bend in the shoreline "—then up the highway to your road."

"Are you going to wear one?"

"Never do."

"Isn't that foolish?" Thea asked. "Aren't they like seat belts?"

"They're like prisons."

Thea finished pulling on the boots and stood with her sandals in her hand. She had a feeling he was testing her again, as if he needed to decide which Thea to believe in: the one who'd fight for him against the whole town or the one who couldn't pick up a dead mouse. More, she sensed he really wanted her to pass the test though he doubted she would.

"I have no wish to go to prison, Damon."

Damon nodded as if she had said the right thing. "Good."

Thea walked awkwardly over to him in the too-big boots. He took her sandals and put them in the little compartment.

"You don't have one of those seat back things."

"Nope," Damon said, straddling the machine. "When I let a woman ride with me, she wants to sit close and hang on to me.'' He flicked up a brow, grinning fiendishly. ''That's usually the point.''

Thea grinned back and slid her hand over the leather. ''No wonder it looks barely used.''

''Touché, Prebble,'' Damon said, laughing. He pushed the starter button and the motor roared. Bending down, he flipped out footrests for Thea on each side of the bike and aimed a thumb at the seat behind him. ''Climb on.''

Relieved she'd worn jeans this morning, Thea put her foot on a pedal and swung her other leg over the back. She wondered absently how girls got on the back of Jerry's motorcycle with that big bar thing in the way. She sat up straight on the surprisingly comfortable seat and grabbed Damon by his belt loops.

He laughed and kicked something. The motorcycle jumped forward suddenly. Thea shrieked and grabbed him around the waist, holding on for dear life.

''That's better,'' Damon hollered over the roar of the bike. ''Now slide up close, so I don't worry about whether you're going to stay on.''

Thea did as he told her. Her thighs wrapped around his buttocks, her arms stayed securely around his hard, warm middle, and her hands squeezed the washboard muscles of his abdomen, so apparent through the cotton of his tank top. Every inch of her front was pressed to his back, her breasts nearly flattened. He was too tall for her to see over, so she turned her head to the side and laid her cheek on his shoulder blade.

''Okay,'' she said, ''I'm ready.''

''I can tell by the relaxed way you're clutching me,'' Damon said. He lifted his foot and the bike sped forward.

Thea tensed even more, tightening her grip, letting not a micrometer of space come between her body and his. The lake sped by beside them, looking dark now beneath the thickening cloud cover.

She turned her head the other way, but the waving yellow-and-blue blur of dandelions and lupines was just as bad. Bits of dust and an occasional insect hit her arms. Wind pulled pins from her hair, and curls flicked her cheeks. A sensation of helplessness assailed her. She felt completely unprotected.

At least, thank heavens, the bike quit jumping. Even when Damon shifted, the ride was smooth. But he did keep shifting, increasing their speed. Feeling that her only security came from him, Thea tried to lean closer. She could only do that by relaxing, letting her body melt against his.

When she quit fighting the bike's motion, something changed. Now she sensed Damon's movements almost before he made them. She began to know when a curve was coming up before she saw it or even felt the bike lean. She closed her eyes, no longer needing a visual anchor.

The fear she'd felt at riding something without sides changed to a feeling of utter freedom. She and Damon and the machine melded into one creature. Even the excessively loud motor seemed to encapsulate them in their own small space.

When Damon slowed the bike, Thea was startled to hear herself murmur, "Don't stop."

Damon chuckled. She couldn't hear it over the roar of the motor, but she felt it beneath her cheek. "There's a Stop sign, Prebble."

Surely, Thea didn't say, "Ignore it," without even lifting her head. She couldn't have. She would never say such a thing.

But Damon must have heard someone say something like that, for the bike surged ahead through the Stop sign and onto the highway. The speed Thea had dreaded only moments ago now shot exhilaration through her veins. She gave Damon a hard squeeze, this time from pure pleasure. She wanted to throw back her head and yell, but she couldn't bring herself to end the contact with his skin and muscle.

When they neared the turn for Auntie's house, Thea tensed. She didn't want to stop; she never wanted to stop. But she couldn't ask Damon to give up even more time from work. He was already missing most of the afternoon to do her a favor.

But Damon must have felt her resistance, for he simply twisted the throttle and sped past the turn. As they continued up the hill away from town, he went faster and faster. Thea had never felt so alive, all her nerves electrified, her senses acutely aware.

The air turned chilly as they rode higher. She shivered slightly, but she didn't want to stop. Not ever. She understood now why Chelsea and Father had so adamantly refused ever to let her ride on a motorcycle. Because this sense of freedom made her want to flee society, break rules, never conform again. And the feeling of union, of oneness, between her body and Damon's would undoubtedly shock Chelsea to her core.

Had Father and Chelsea known this would happen? Did it happen to everyone, or was Thea succumbing again to that relentless Prebble gene? She wondered if Dora had ever ridden motorcycles. If so, surely she'd loved it.

Thunder cracked overhead and the clouds opened. Raindrops hit Thea's arms and legs like cold bullets. The rest of her, protected by Damon's broad body, simply got drenched.

"Oooh, brr," Thea exclaimed.

"An understatement," Damon muttered.

Thea realized he was slowing. "Don't stop," she said. "It f-f-feels wonderful."

"Yeah, right," Damon said, pulling the bike into the parking overlook near the top of the hill. Rain clouds obscured the view. "I can tell you're not cold at all. Grab that saddlebag behind the seat for me."

She had to slide back on the seat to reach the leather bag and began shivering in earnest when she let go of Damon's body. He took a leather jacket from the bag. Still holding the bike upright between his thighs, he held the jacket while she stuck her arms in it, then zipped it up.

"It *is* s-sort of cold out," she said with a shiver.

Damon reached toward her head and ran his fingers through her dripping hair. "Your schoolteacher's bun has come loose," he said, grinning. "Thank God." He pulled one long curl down in front of her eyes. "All corkscrewed up like when you were a kid. It's a big improvement."

"Just don't g-g-go back to calling me Orphan Annie."

"Not a chance. 'Prebble' says so much more about you."

"M-m-more? What d-d-do you mean?"

Damon's brow shot up. "Did you like the ride, Prebble?"

"Yes, so f-f-far."

He nodded. "Exactly. Now, hang on, I'd better get you home before you freeze."

"A hot sh-shower," she chattered.

"Are you inviting me to join you in one?" He gave her his sexy devil's grin, but she didn't see his usual taunting in it.

In her chilled state, she couldn't summon the imperiousness to respond to his suggestion as Chelsea would have expected. She couldn't have carried it off well anyway because, for some reason, she found herself smiling—as much as she could with her lips stiff from cold.

Besides, she had no desire to argue right then. All she could think of was getting her cold body once again pressed tightly against Damon's.

Without hesitation, she slid back up the seat and wrapped her body around his.

CHAPTER SEVEN

DAMON parked his bike as close as he could to the front porch, but wind blew rain beneath the overhang. Grabbing Thea around the waist, he helped her off the bike. They ran up the steps, then turned together and watched the rain pelt the earth and his motorcycle.

Thea leaned against him, completely at ease, liking the feel of his arm around her waist, the strength in his man's body. But the moment passed quickly. Her sense of letting go, of freedom, dissipated as she stood on Auntie's porch. She had too much work to do here to continue ignoring reality.

Sighing, she straightened away from Damon, already missing the wildness of the ride. But she knew, even from her brief experience, that it was too intoxicating to indulge in often. She shivered. It was also too cold.

Damon turned to open the door. "Better get into something warm and dry."

"Warm and wet," Thea corrected him. "Like a hot shower." She glanced again at the rain. "You should come in and dry off, Damon. You can't ride in this weather, can you?"

"Not if I can help it," he admitted. "But I doubt you've got anything here I can put on."

Thea looked at his broad shoulders and had to agree. "How about a towel?"

"That'll work." In the hall, he urged her down on the bench and tugged off her boots. When she went up the stairs, he headed for the kitchen. "Want coffee?" he asked.

106

"Sounds lovely," she said. "Do you know where everything is?"

Damon cocked a brow. "Better than you probably."

He acted so at home here, so *un*guestlike, Thea felt wrapped up in coziness, rather the way the noise of the engine had enveloped her on the ride. But she had a feeling that enjoying it might turn out to be as risky as riding motorcycles.

"I'll get you that towel," she said, hurrying up the stairs.

She found the largest, thickest towel she could in the linen closet and went to the top of the stairs to toss it down to him. Damon had already removed his shirt. He stood in the hallway downstairs. Thea's breath caught in her throat; her arm froze in midtoss.

The man was beautiful. In the dim gray light, shadows highlighted the sinews in his chest, the rippling stomach muscles she'd felt through his T-shirt on their ride. His black hair and the wet black jeans clinging to his long legs contrasted with his bronze skin, making it appear silky smooth. Thea felt her bare feet begin to move toward the top of the steps as if they planned to carry her down the stairs, to let her hands discover if all that skin felt as satiny as it looked.

With a shake of her head, she dispelled the thought and threw the towel. What on earth had one ride on a motorcycle done to her brain?

She turned toward Dora's room and stopped. Dear heaven, she couldn't go in *there*. That's how this whole afternoon had started!

"Damon," she called. "Can you...?"

Could she ask him to put his shirt on before he came upstairs? A cold, icky wet shirt that had gotten that way because *Thea* had worn his leather jacket? Indeed, she could not.

"Can I what?" he hollered.

"The mouse is still in there," she wailed.

His laughter resounded up the stairway. His feet followed a moment later. "Did you check?" he asked as he reached the hall.

Thea knew he was walking toward her, all of him, but she saw only the sinews and silky skin of his bare chest. "Check?" she asked, confused.

"To see if it's still on your bed."

He wiggled his brows in that Dracula way, obviously trying to scare her. Thea barely noticed. By now, he stood so close to her, his warmth touched her. She could hardly swallow. *Get a grip*, she admonished herself, backing up a step.

"Maybe they finished it off after you left. Devoured the whole bloody—"

"Damon!" He turned and Thea gasped again. "Damon, what…?"

On his back, done in shades of black, was a large tattoo of a fierce standing grizzly, his front paws extended, claws unsheathed, his teeth bared. Below the bear, in letters so small Thea had to lean close to read them, it said, "Running Bear."

"Oh," Thea said, "I…that's your name."

"One of 'em." Damon turned to face her. Her fingers sliding over the words made her realize she had put her hand on his back. "My mother's part Blackfoot."

"It's *her* name?" Thea's lips formed these mundane words while her mind thought only of touching his warm skin again.

"It sure as hell ain't my father's." A sneer came into his voice whenever he spoke of his father. "And the name's about all I got from my mother."

"Oh, that's not true, Damon. She gave you…" Thea couldn't help herself—she touched her hand to his chest. A muscle jumped beneath her palm, making her realize what she was doing. She snatched her hand away. "She gave you...a heritage you should be proud of."

"Oh, I'm proud, Prebble. Damn proud, actually." He cupped her chin as if to force her attention, but his touch was so gentle she barely felt the calluses on his skin. Just his warmth. "My ancestors fought the system, too—just like me."

"You don't always need to fight so hard, you know."

He lifted one naked bronze shoulder. "It's what's inside me, Prebble." He gave her a suggestive grin. "And until you think you can handle the inside, you'd better keep your greedy fingers off my outside." He leaned close to whisper warmly in her ear, "If you think you can."

Thea expelled a breath meant to sound disgusted, but it came out a shaky sigh. "I can assure you, Damon, I'll have no trouble at all."

She stuck her hands behind her back, then realized she must look exactly like a little kid ordered not to touch something she could barely resist. She jammed them on her hips instead.

Damon laughed till she ground her teeth, then turned and entered Dora's room.

A minute later, he emerged holding a tiny corpse by the tail. "Care to say something Christian over the—"

Thea fled into the room and slammed the door. But even the thick oak couldn't drown out Damon's laughter.

In the shower, despite the soothing effects of hot water, Thea couldn't get rid of her awareness that Damon, half-dressed, waited downstairs. Nor could she entirely dispel that tingling sense of freedom she'd had on the ride.

She toweled her hair, but left it down, curling wildly, not wanting to take the time to dry it. Much as she wanted to snuggle into her thick terry robe, she left it hanging in the closet. Proper daytime clothes would create a far safer atmosphere.

Thea pulled on a pair of leggings and a soft fleece tunic, mentally admonishing herself to heed the message she wanted to send Damon. If *she* did, it wouldn't matter whether he understood it or not. Besides, he hadn't been the one standing in the hallway ogling her—it had been the other way around.

She shook her head again, still stunned at her response to Damon's naked torso. Thea had never felt stirrings like that before.

Oh, she had seen good-looking men before, and even admired their physiques. But *ogled*? Never—never before half an hour ago. She'd known the difference immediately, when her whole body had joined her eyes in reacting to Damon.

To Damon's body.

And, unfortunately, she'd also known at once exactly what such behavior meant. Despite Father's and Chelsea's best efforts, despite her own near absolute conformance to their rules, the thing they'd feared the most had happened. Heredity had won: she was just like her mother.

One ride on a motorcycle, one taste of freedom, one look at that man's impossibly gorgeous, hunky chest, and twenty-four years of breeding and reserve crumbled. She was...a sex maniac.

Well, she wouldn't permit it. She had recognized it in plenty of time to keep it from ruining her life, as it had her mother's and to some extent even Dora's.

Of course she liked Damon. How could she not? He was a little rough sometimes, but he'd been very kind to her since she arrived.

But Thea had no intention of making her mother's oft-repeated mistake and confusing sexual desire with love. Thea couldn't deny Damon's sex appeal, but she could resist it.

She touched her fingertips to her cheeks and found them

flushed and hot. A quick peek in the mirror told her she didn't need blush this evening.

Downstairs, Thea checked the kitchen, the den, then all the closed-off rooms, wondering where Damon had gone. Had he recognized her reaction upstairs in the hall—no doubt when she trailed her fingers over his tattoo—and escaped while she was in the shower? Resisting him would be easy if he planned to avoid her. But when she looked out the window, his motorcycle still stood near the porch getting drenched in the rain.

Returning to the kitchen, she noticed the door to the basement was open. Thea hadn't gone down there yet. Perhaps now would be a good time. Having Damon with her might make seeing Auntie's workroom less painful.

She started down the well-lit stairs. Very well-lit, Thea noted. Auntie must have had these fixtures installed as her eyes aged. Going down the steps, Thea counted six lights. They certainly dispelled the gloom of the basement.

At the bottom of the stairs, a closed door on the left led to Auntie's workroom. To the right was a big storage space, larger than the front parlor and kitchen combined, and off that was the door to the laundry room. Hearing noises there, Thea picked her way toward it, stepping around and over boxes and old pieces of furniture most would consider junk. Without Auntie, they were likely to remain junk.

Opening the door to the laundry room, Thea gave a little shriek. "Oh, Damon! I..." She shut her eyes, but her lids immediately popped open again.

Damon shot her an ironic glance. Dressed in only the towel, which he had knotted around his middle, he sat on top of the humming dryer, obviously waiting for the machine to finish drying his clothes. *All* his clothes.

"I'm sorry," Thea said, backing out of the room, her gaze firmly focused on the floor. "I had no idea."

"I'm sure you didn't, Prebble." Damon didn't sound

embarrassed at all. He made no move to cover himself more than he already was. Which wasn't much. "I doubt if you came down here hoping to catch me in my altogether." He chuckled that irresistible chuckle. "Or you wouldn't have given me such a big towel."

"Oh, honestly," she said. "Couldn't you have at least kept on your underwear?"

He met her uncomfortable gaze for the second she flicked it over him. Just long enough to see he was enjoying himself thoroughly.

He softened his voice. "What makes you think I wear underwear?"

"Damon Free!"

Turning, Thea pushed open the door. Thunder cracked overhead, sending its rumbling noise all the way to the basement. The six bright lights over the stairs flickered and went out. The dryer stopped.

Thea froze.

How on earth was she going to get across that cluttered room without breaking her leg? She took a step, barked her shin on something and cried out.

"Better wait till the lights come on," Damon said close behind her. He took her upper arms and turned her back into the darkened laundry room, where the smell of detergent and warmth from the dryer surrounded her. "It usually only takes a minute or two."

Thea was trembling like a leaf in the wind and praying hard. Praying that Damon didn't know why she was trembling.

"I can't wait in here with you," she said. "It wouldn't be proper."

"No kidding," Damon said agreeably. "It's a little late for that, don't you think?"

Thea bit her lip. He knew, he knew. "What do you mean?"

"What was so damn proper about your ride on my bike? Speeding, running Stop signs, letting your hair down, putting your body as close to mine as you could with your clothes still on?" His tone was lazy, not judgmental as Chelsea's would have been.

Thea said nothing. She couldn't disagree. And she didn't want to add weight to his arguments by agreeing.

"Come sit on the dryer," he said, urging her into the room and letting the door shut behind them. "It's nice and warm. And you're shaking again."

In a few steps, he turned her around to face him, found her waist with his hands and lifted her onto the dryer.

"You're not cold are you?"

"No, I just—"

"You really scared of the dark? Even when you know the sun's shining up there somewhere above the clouds?"

"I'm not scared of the dark."

Damon found her shoulders with his hands and squeezed softly. "Then why are you trembling?"

Thea shrugged her shoulders trying to dislodge him, but it didn't work. "I'm just upset by...this situation. I don't feel..." She bit her lip again. "You wouldn't understand."

"Try me." His voice was gentle, not teasing. "I figured out yesterday there may be more to you than I know. Now's a good time for you to fill me in—in the dark, where I can't see you blushing."

"You don't have to pretend to be interested," Thea said, surprised. The men she dated talked about themselves, not her.

Damon hesitated. "I'm not pretending, Prebble." He ran his hands down her arms to her hands. "I'm curious. Much as I hate to admit it, maybe I was wrong all these years."

"It's just..." Thea took a long breath full of shudders. "Events seem to be making my decisions for me. I'm used to staying in control. It's what I was taught, the way I feel safe.'' She wanted to touch his face, feel to see if he was laughing at her though he wasn't making any noise. She tucked her hands under her thighs. ''*You* ride your motorcycle every day. You're used to the way it makes you feel. I'm not. I didn't expect that, all that…''

''Like you don't care about anything but how good it feels right then?''

''Yes, exactly. I didn't even care about the rain. Except it made me cold.'' She let out a big breath. ''So cold I took a shower when you had your shirt off, which is simply not the kind of thing I do.''

''I wasn't in the shower with you, Prebble,'' Damon said, his voice deeper somehow, no doubt choking on amusement. ''Though I'd have been glad to join you if you wanted.''

''No, no, you know I don't mean that,'' she said quickly. ''But you were…very close. And the rain made you the same way.''

''Made me the same *what*?'' Damon asked. Now he was laughing. ''If you think I was worried about your taking a shower—''

''No, it made you cold and wet.'' Her words came faster, tumbling out before she could think them through. ''I can't tell you to sit and shiver while I get warm and dry. But the way you're dressed…'' Of their own volition, her hands left the restraint of her legs and fluttered over his chest. ''Not dressed at all.'' His skin felt just as it did over his tattoo, like silk. Silk stretched tightly over steel. ''I don't…never…''

''It's not like we're on Main Street,'' Damon said softly.

''But I'm sitting here with you—'' her voice wobbled up and down a couple of octaves ''—just as though it's the proper thing to do. As though…I *like* it. As though I want to stay…want you to… Damon?''

Damon made a noise then, but it wasn't a word. More

like a growl, but not an angry one. Like…like he wanted to eat her.

"Damon?"

His strong hands covered her knees and pushed them apart.

"Damon, I'm not sure… Do you think we ought…" She put her hands on his chest and held him away. Sort of.

"Ought?" he said quietly, as if he'd never heard the word before. "Oh, yeah, we ought."

Insinuating his body between her legs, he wrapped his arms around her waist. Her feeble resistance collapsed as he pulled her traitorously willing body against his chest.

"Oh, Damon, oh. I…"

His lips found her ear and nibbled the lobe as his tongue traced tantalizing patterns around the whorls. Her head tipped toward him as if begging for more.

"What do you think, Prebble?" he breathed. "Do you want me to stop?"

Stop? What on earth was he saying? Her mind couldn't grasp his meaning, so she let her body answer. "No, no, Damon, please—"

He cut off her words with his mouth. If the skin of his chest felt like silk, his lips felt like velvet, warm, soft, wet velvet. Soothingly luxurious, frantically delicious. A taste she'd known only once before, a taste that filled her with hunger for more.

Instinctively, greedily, she nibbled at his lips, running her tongue over them, leaning into him. He slanted his open mouth over hers, taking her lips inside his, then urging them apart. His tongue probed and retreated, probed and retreated.

Sensation swamped her, making her barely aware of her movements. She knew only the craving Damon had ignited in her. Longing to get closer, to touch more of him, Thea arched, flattening her breasts against his chest. Her nipples pebbled from the pressure. She heard a desperate moaning sound and knew it was too female to have come from Damon. It must have come from her throat. Or her chest. For she had not lifted her mouth from his. Much as she needed deeper breaths of air, she never wanted their mouths to separate.

Damon drew back. "Thea, God," he gasped, his voice scratchy. "Do you know what you're doing to me?"

"No," she almost cried. "How could I?" Her chest heaved rapidly, drawing in air in gulps. "I only know what's happening to me."

And it wouldn't happen, it couldn't, she understood all too clearly now, except with Damon. Everything she'd mastered about controlling men, all the tricks she'd practiced to keep them at a prudent distance—none of them worked with Damon. Because with Damon, she could not control herself.

With a slight crackle, the lights flickered on. "Damon!" Thea gasped. "You're naked."

He glanced down at the towel on the floor. "So I am. It didn't seem to matter in the dark." He grinned unrepentantly. "Want me to put it back on? Or do you just think I 'ought'?"

Thea jumped off the dryer. As a method of escape, it was disastrous. She slid down Damon's hard, unclothed body and landed on the floor, shaking with the sensations shooting along her nerves, trapped between him and the steel machine.

"No, Damon." She fought for control. "It may be way too late for propriety, but it's too darn early for this." When she pushed his chest, he moved easily out of her way.

Freed, she ran from the laundry room, stumbled across the cluttered storage room as fast as she could and fled up the stairs. She didn't stop in the kitchen but continued up the wide staircase to Dora's room and threw herself on the bed.

She lay on her stomach a moment, then turned onto her back and stared at a crack in the ceiling. She tried to think of something, anything besides what she'd nearly done with Damon Free on top of the dryer. But she couldn't. The throbbing ache of dissatisfaction low in her belly wouldn't let her think of anything else.

Gradually, the frantic side to her wanting calmed. She could think almost clearly. But she couldn't understand her behavior...nor her words.

Dear heaven, when Damon had asked her if she wanted him to stop, why hadn't she said, of course you should stop, Mr. Free? Step back and take your hands off my knees. The man had stood between her thighs, had pressed his body to hers—and what had she done? She'd *begged* him to continue!

Thea flopped back onto her stomach. She made herself a solemn vow. No matter how much she wanted to, she would never again ride with Damon on his motorcycle.

Another unrelated thought flitted through her mind. She had judged her mother too harshly all these years. She rolled onto her back. One couldn't fight one's DNA. Some people inherited big brains, some inherited big muscles, others got stuck with an insatiable craving for the wrong man.

Damon knocked on the doorjamb since Thea hadn't bothered to shut the door. "Thea?"

She covered her eyes with her hand. "Damon, I don't want to see you right now. Can we talk tomorrow?"

"If that's what you want." He sounded concerned. She heard his footsteps approach the bed and she pulled herself to the other side. "I'm not going to hurt you, for God's sake."

"Oh, I trust *you* implicitly," she said. "Though for my sake I'm glad you've put your clothes on."

"Are you being sarcastic?"

Thea lifted herself on her elbows. "I must not do it as well as you, since you didn't recognize it right away."

Damon didn't smile. "Are you all right?"

"Of course I'm all right," Thea said. "It was just a simple kiss after all."

"Like hell!" Damon said. "It was more like the kiss of the decade. Maybe the century." Heat glowed in his dangerous dark eyes. "You may as well admit it."

"I'll admit no such thing."

The base of Thea's spine seemed to be melting. Now didn't seem like the time to mention that she hadn't been kissing for a whole decade. Of course, even Damon hadn't been kissing for a century. Did that mean he'd kissed a hundred women? And…*this* kiss—the kiss he'd just shared with "proper Theadora Birch"—had outdone them all? Trembles quivered all through her. Dear heaven, she truly was a Prebble.

Thea drew herself into a sitting position. "I'm sorry I behaved like an idiot. I was just…taken by surprise."

"Yeah," he agreed. "The day's been filled with surprises." He waited for her to meet his gaze. "If you think *I* was prepared for what just happened downstairs, think again."

He gazed at her for a long moment. She returned the look without flinching, saying nothing.

"Okay," he said at last. He aimed a thumb downstairs. "I left hot chocolate for you on the stove. And I fed your cats so you don't need to worry about it."

"Thank you," she said, gazing over his shoulder.

"I checked the phone. It's working." He put a fingertip under her chin. "So call me if you need anything. I wrote my numbers by the phone in the kitchen."

"That's kind of you, but I'm sure I won't need a thing."
She longed for him to remove his finger, but it felt too
good, calluses and all, to lift her jaw away from the contact.

"I'll stop by in the morning," Damon said. "Bring you
a steamer to get the old wallpaper off. Shouldn't take you
more than a week."

"Right," Thea said. "Good idea. That and cleaning."

Damon nodded. "Be good for you." He turned and left.

Thea let out the long breath she'd been holding and
slumped into the pillow.

Damon stuck his head and shoulders back through the
doorway. "It had to happen sometime."

She lifted her head. "Well, it won't happen again, Mr.
Free."

He flicked up that annoyingly male eyebrow. "Care to
put money on that, Ms. Prebble?"

This time when he left, he was laughing.

"Sleep tight," he called from outside, just before his
motorcycle roared to life, drowning all other sound.

Thea leapt off the bed and began pacing the room. No
wonder the darn man had a child out of wedlock. She was
surprised he didn't have dozens all over the valley. Maybe
he did, for all she knew. Perhaps she'd be finding out about
them for years to come.

But why on earth would she? It was none of *her* business
how many women he'd bedded in the past. Or for that
matter, how many women he'd bedded since this morning.
He wasn't her lover! She shouldn't forget that. He was her
contractor. A friend of her aunt's. He could make love to
whomever he wished.

On her fourth or fifth circuit of the room, Thea quit lying
to herself. A few seconds of stark self-honesty halted her
steps and left her thunderstruck in the middle of the room.

She had every reason to be jealous of Roni. Beautiful
Roni: tall and dark-haired, the kind of complexion Thea'd

always dreamed of having. One that tanned instead of turning bright red. Thick, straight brown hair, instead of carrot red corkscrews. And big brown eyes so liquid and sweet, the woman could probably overcharge every male who came through her checkout line and none would ever notice.

And Darlene, with the big feet, who got to leave her boots with Damon because she knew she'd be back.

And that pretty blonde the other day, who didn't mind snuggling up to him in view of the whole town.

Thea was jealous of them all.

Because Thea was in love with Damon Free.

She loved his kind heart, his passion for loyalty, his teasing; she loved his adolescent rebel's attitude toward life; she even loved his tattoo. She loved his callused hands, his velvet lips, his silky skin. Especially she loved the way he'd always cared for Dora.

She loved the way he'd acted today *after* their kiss. He'd been shaken, too—he'd admitted it. But all his concern had been for Thea.

And Lord knew she loved kissing Damon.

She loved everything about him. Except maybe his work ethic. And the way he treated his son.

Thea staggered over to Dora's window seat. Something didn't make sense. How could a man who felt as Damon did about loyalty, who had returned to a town that despised him simply to care for an elderly friend, desert a child? How could a man with Damon's view of friendship let a friend do the bulk of the work on a house for which, presumably, they were both receiving pay?

She rubbed her eyes, trying to see answers instead of confusion. But her tired mind couldn't part the fog. Much as she loved him, there were many things about Damon she didn't understand yet. But she would—and soon.

She had only two weeks till the city council meeting.

Then she'd have to convince seven people that Damon was the man her heart believed—not the man they'd known for nearly three decades.

CHAPTER EIGHT

THEA wasn't sure what woke her. A sound that didn't quite belong. Not the cats, for they were curled comfortably on her bed.

She slitted open an eye to look at the clock. Good heavens, it was eight-thirty. She never slept past six on a weekday at home. In fact, since she was a child, she'd never felt relaxed enough to sleep in—except when she visited Auntie.

Of course, she hadn't gotten to bed until nearly 4:00 a.m. But she'd completed the audit she'd promised her boss at her old C.P.A. firm and sent it to him over the Internet. Her mouth felt like a desert and her eyes like sandpaper, but it was a schedule she'd better get used to if she planned to finish this restoration with her head financially above water—or even near the surface.

Thea heard the noise again, and this time it was quite clear where it came from: her doorway.

"Time to get your fanny out of bed, Prebble," Damon said, knocking again on the jamb.

"Damon," Thea protested, her voice somewhere between groan and yawn, "*what* are you doing in my bedroom?"

"I phoned," he said. "When you didn't answer, I wondered if you'd come to your senses and left town. I knocked downstairs—for ten minutes. You sleep like the dead, Prebble. Besides, I'm not in your bedroom, I'm in the hallway. But if you're not outta that bed in five minutes..." He flicked up an eyebrow suggestively.

Thea rolled onto her stomach, stretching and arching her

back. "Okay, okay. Just…" She dropped her head back onto the pillow. "Didn't I lock the doors last night?"

Damon shook his head. "Your mind must have been distracted by all those lustful thoughts you—"

"Get out of here, Damon!" Thea threw a pillow at him.

Laughing, he disappeared from her doorway. "Five minutes."

Thea rolled over and looked at the sun-washed ceiling, grinning foolishly. It wasn't such a bad way to wake up, she thought, rubbing her hands up and down her back and wondering what Damon's hands would feel like there, rubbing, at this hour of the morning. Wouldn't his strong hands wake her up even more nicely than his deep voice?

Afraid of pursuing such thoughts in her unclothed state with Damon only a few steps away, Thea rose and dressed—more or less. A few minutes later, she straggled downstairs in her old pink sweats. Damon met her in the hallway with a mug of coffee and nodded toward the front porch.

Thea followed without thinking, until she reached the front door. Rules and reason set in as she glanced down at her baggy sweats, ran a hand over her frizzy hair. Then she shrugged.

This was Montana, not Virginia. She could sit with Damon out on her porch, improperly dressed, too early in the morning, and no one would know or care. As she followed him outside, she wondered if it was really the sheltering hills of her new state that made her feel so comfortable—or her companion?

On the porch, Damon swung the wicker chair around so she could see the sun glistening on the lake but wouldn't have the glare in her eyes. He ran a hand over the back. "You cleaned this up?"

"Mmm-hmm," Thea agreed. "And fixed the leg so it doesn't wobble."

Damon wiggled the chair skeptically. "Maybe this restoration has a chance after all."

"Thank you," she said. "I think."

He sat on the railing, which tipped beneath his weight. "You didn't get to the railing, I see."

She took the mug he held out to her. "Good morning, Damon. This is very nice. Do you cater luncheons, too? Or just these early-morning affairs?" She curled her feet beneath her.

Damon's expression softened and his lids dropped lower over his eyes. "'Affairs' early in the morning?" he said huskily. "Hey, if I'd known you were in the mood, I'd never have waited in the hall." He cupped her chin. "Whenever you want it, Prebble, just let me know. I'll fit you into my busy schedule somehow."

His hand felt so good on her skin, Thea felt the warmth all through her. But she was still too relaxed from sleep to let his teasing rile her. "You are so funny, Damon."

"Few would agree with you." As he continued to let his gaze roam over her face, his smile turned to a frown. "You look like hell this morning, Prebble."

"Thanks so much, Damon." She turned her head, dislodging his hand.

"What'd you do, stay up all night wishing I was here?"

Thea took another sip of coffee, hoping to dispel the clouds from her brain. "Much as I hate to encourage your already inflated ego, I'd have vastly preferred your company to what I did last night, Damon." She explained about her arrangement to keep doing audits over the Internet.

Damon's frown deepened. "How long do you think you can keep up that kind of schedule?" he asked. "Working all night, then trying to get something done during the day. You're nuts, Prebble. You'll get sick or something. Or injure yourself with a tool."

"How sweet that you're worried about me," Thea said.

Damon—worried about her? She wanted to purr like one of her cats. "Why don't you tell me what brings you here this hour of the morning?"

After another long glare at her, Damon shrugged and leaned down to pick up a heavy-looking mechanical contraption. "I brought this wallpaper steamer over for you. Remember? I told you I'd be here this morning."

"I didn't realize morning meant the crack of dawn," Thea said.

Damon rolled his eyes. "That's what Dora used to call 10:00 a.m., too."

Thea pushed back a corkscrew of hair that had escaped from the halfhearted ponytail she'd stuffed it into. "I don't, except here," she said. "It's the only place I was ever allowed to sleep in when I was little. Father believes in getting up with the sun."

Damon laughed. "Dora hadn't seen a sunrise in about fifty years. That's why I put in all those lights for her down the stairs. She liked to work at night."

"You did a lot for her, didn't you?" Thea asked. "I'm so glad she had you, Damon."

Damon's eyes darkened in that way that hid his emotions. "We did a lot for each other," he said. "There isn't any question in my mind who did more." He raised a shoulder in a shrug. "Mostly, we were just friends."

"How'd you meet her?" Thea asked.

"I came here one day with a kid from school." Damon gazed into the distance. "She always had a bunch of kids here, right up until she died. This kid from my shop class told her I was good with tools and could fix her wobbly front step." He smiled as if remembering. "She was so good with furniture and never bothered with things around the house."

Damon had never sounded so comfortable with Thea before. She prayed he wouldn't stop talking. "So you fixed the step, and she gave you milk and cookies, and you saw that was better than pot, and you—''

"Not exactly, Prebble," Damon said, but he was still smiling. Even his eyes were warm, not troubling to hide the love he'd felt for Dora.

"It wasn't that easy, you mean?"

"Yeah," he agreed. "But basically, you about described it." He gave her an assessing look as if trying to decide whether he could trust her. "You know Dora smoked pot with me once?"

"Dora?" Thea exclaimed. "She didn't!"

"She did," Damon said. "Wanted to show me how dumb people act stoned."

"Did it work?"

"When we quit laughing," Damon said. "But not the way she thought. I didn't think she looked dumb at all. I thought she looked damned amazing. I mean, here was this seventy-year-old woman I barely knew willing to get arrested to help me. It was…"

"An awakening experience?" Thea prompted.

Damon nodded. "That's an understatement. Anyway, that's what I mean if you tote it up, she did a helluva lot more for me than I could ever do for her. Like that first time—I fixed her step and she fixed my life. Pretty uneven, wouldn't you say?"

Thea shook her head. "No, I wouldn't say that, and I bet Dora wouldn't, either. She loved you. I doubt she was keeping score."

"Yeah," Damon said quietly. "The only one in town."

He was looking at Thea vaguely, but not as though he saw her—more as if he'd forgotten she was there. Or at least had forgotten who she was. Thea wondered if last night's flare of emotion and desire had anything to do with the side of Damon she was seeing this morning.

She just wanted it to last longer.

"The only one in town who didn't keep score, Damon?" Thea asked. "Or the only one who loved you?"

Damon's charcoal-dark eyes came to rest on Thea, seeming to suddenly come into focus. "Both," he said shortly.

Pushing himself off the railing, he strode to the end of the porch and stared out over the lake at the mountains. Dora's view. Thea looked at the tension in his strong back and saw mistrust returning.

"What did you do to make the rest of the town judge you so harshly?" She stood and walked quietly down the porch.

"Nothing," he spat. "Most of this town wrote me off the day I was born. My mother was one of Dad's ranch hands, just passing through. After she had his baby, she left me with him and kept passing through. Dad was bitter and didn't want a kid. He didn't try to hide it."

Thea's chest ached with sadness at the thought of Damon growing up without a mother. She remembered how lonely she'd felt the year her mother divorced her father. But at least she'd always known where her mother was; she could write to her, see her now and then. No wonder Dora had responded so quickly and deeply to this troubled boy.

"Damon, I'm sorry."

"Don't waste your time," he growled. He kept his back to her, arms crossed tightly across his chest as if holding something in. "I had your aunt. By the time I met her, my old man had written me off completely. So I practically moved in with Dora."

"Why didn't you?"

"Dad was nasty, not stupid," Damon said. "You think he'd give up a free ranch hand?"

"Is he still in Pine Butte?" Thea asked. "Do you see him often?"

"See him?" Damon spun around. "Are you kidding? I haven't seen him for five...six years. Why would I?"

"Damon," Thea exclaimed, "your own father?"

"Don't give me that sunny-sweet crap about fathers, Prebble," Damon said. "He sired me, nothing more." Fury etched his face. "Know why my old man quit beating me?" He glared at her as if she was dragging these admissions from him against his will. But he didn't stop. And he couldn't force his voice to maintain the cold, neutral tone he usually used. "One reason. I got stronger than him. The bastard didn't think he'd enjoy it as much if I took the belt away from him."

"Oh, Damon." Something in his voice made her want to cry. She took his face between her palms, longing to soothe him; aching to take back her platitude about fathers and offer comfort instead. "Damon, I—"

He shook her hands off and spun away from her. "It happened a long time ago, Thea. To lots of kids. Don't worry about it."

Not letting herself think about her actions, Thea took a step toward him and slid her hands around his waist. Holding on tight, she pressed her cheek to his back, just as she had on the motorcycle. He stiffened as if to move away, but she latched her hands together over his hard stomach.

"Don't you ever let anyone see inside you?"

Gradually, she felt the tension ease in him a tiny bit. "Only Dora." Suddenly, he turned in her arms and squeezed her hard against him. "Till now."

He stood, holding her, breathing as hard as if he'd just run a race. When he seemed to calm, he kissed the top of her head. As platonic as the touch was, it started frissons of pleasure swirling inside her. She tightened her grip around his waist.

"It was a helluva lot easier to understand my feelings for her," Damon said. "She was old enough to be my grandmother. I never felt any of this stuff—" he nuzzled

Thea's ear, kissed down her throat till her head tipped toward him "—for Dora."

"I'm glad to hear it," Thea said, forcing herself to stay on the subject. "I think that sort of crush would have been emotionally unhealthy for you."

He chuckled his devastating chuckle. Finally, he took a deep breath. His chest expanded against her breasts, making them feel achy and heavy.

"Want to learn how to use that steamer?"

"I can hardly wait," Thea lied.

She doubted she'd hear a word he said about the device, but she feared staying in his arms another second. Her reaction to him this time went far past simple physical desire.

The wounded side Damon had let her see, though he obviously hadn't meant to, touched her deeply. Wrapped in his arms, she loved feeling protected by his physical strength. But she also wanted to enclose him in an emotional embrace that would shield him from any other hurts. She wished everyone in Pine Butte could see this part of Damon that he hid from most of the world.

The intensity of the emotions swirling through her made rational thought difficult. But she didn't get the feeling that Damon felt as swept away as she did—he certainly hadn't mentioned falling in love with her. So she doubted he'd want to hear such words from her. But if she didn't get free of his arms, that's exactly what she would tell him.

Gathering her strength, Thea stepped back from Damon. "Yes, the steamer," she said unsteadily. "Good idea."

"Right." *His* voice didn't shake at all.

Damon walked back down the porch. Without meeting her eyes, he gave her a few minutes' instruction on the machine. It didn't look hard, just unwieldy. When he raised his gaze to hers, his eyes and expression had regained the neutral shield they usually hid behind.

"There's something else. I should have told you before.'' He spoke quickly, tonelessly, as if he wanted to get the words out and over with before she said anything.

Thea's stomach clenched. He sounded dreadfully somber. ''What now, Damon? Is this about my license? I can't face any more bad news. Tell me tomorrow.''

''Nothing about that.'' He bent over to put the steamer down—or so he didn't have to look her in the eye. ''I can't let you pay me for my labor,'' he said to the decking.

''Pay you? Of *course* I'll—''

''No!'' he said quietly, but with absolute emphasis. ''I promised Dora.'' He straightened. ''Not that I knew what I was promising, exactly. I rode with her in the ambulance. She wasn't making sense, couldn't talk well. But she said something about her will and wanting me to do something. I promised her, whatever it was, I'd do it.''

''Oh, Damon, surely she wouldn't expect—''

His impatient gaze and the cutting motion of his palm through the air stopped her words. ''At the reading, when Silas asked me to be executor, I thought that was it. Then when he read her letter to me…I was stunned.'' He closed his eyes in a deep frown. ''I reacted…overreacted.''

''No, you didn't, Damon. Not at all.'' She bit her lip. ''Dora's gone, and this is way too much for me to ask.''

''You didn't ask,'' he said. ''Dora did. On her deathbed, Prebble. And I gave her my word.''

He walked toward his truck. With her jaw still agape, her mind a swirl, it took Thea a few seconds to realize he was leaving. She chased him down the steps.

''Damon, you—''

His pickup roared to life. He stuck his head out the window. ''Get to work on the wallpaper, hear me, Prebble? You've got a helluva lot to get done this summer. And if you don't want to cut some limb off, you'd better sleep at night. You need an alarm clock. I'll buy you one.''

Before she could answer, he drove off.

*   *   *

Four hours later, Thea put down the steamer and rubbed her arm. The machine hadn't felt all that heavy this morning when Damon showed her how to use it. But holding it up for—she looked at her watch—nearly four hours, with one arm then the other, was a greater strain than six sets of tennis, her previous conception of exercise burnout.

She leaned down to flick off the device and decided to sit down instead. Slumping on the top step, she pushed damp hair out of her face and looked down the stairway. Pride filled her. She had removed two layers of wallpaper in the entry hall and three up the stairs in just one morning.

As she pulled her hand away from her head, she wondered why she'd wasted time showering before she began working. Her hair dripped with wallpaper paste and sweat. She could feel bits of paper stuck in her curls but couldn't get them out without a mirror. And she couldn't get to a mirror without standing up.

Good as she felt about what she'd accomplished, she wondered how many days she could keep up this pace. Especially if she planned to keep doing the auditing she'd promised her boss. Damon's too-generous, too-tempting offer meant she could cut back on her night work. If the offer she'd had the other day on her Corvette came through, she'd be home free. Well, not really free, but she'd make it without mortgaging her land.

But it seemed so unfair to Damon. Not that he'd asked her opinion in the matter.

Closing her eyes, she decided to think about all that later. When she heard the hesitant knock at the front door, she kept them closed. The only person she was interested in seeing was Damon, and if he bothered to knock, it wouldn't sound like that.

Jerry's voice called through the screen. "Thea, is that you? Are you all right?"

Thea forced open her eyes. "Jerry? Come in, please."

She pushed herself up with a hand against the now-bare wall. "I'm just tired from using this steamer of Damon's all morning."

Jerry looked around the entry hall as Thea came down the stairs toward him. "You did all this in one morning...all the way up the stairs?"

"Yes, only I think I need a ride to the hospital," she said, trying not to whine, "so I can get my arms amputated."

"I bet," he said. "You ever do this kind of work before?"

Thea shook her head.

"I think you're supposed to take it a little easy at first, you know?"

Thea smiled weakly. "I wish you'd told me that before I started. Would you like a cup of coffee?"

"If it's made," Jerry said. "I really need to get back to the job site. I'm just looking for Damon. I couldn't raise him on the cell phone, and I think this new plumber's cutting corners. Damon'd fry him if he knew. The guy's never worked for him before, but Damon's got the two plumbers he usually works with on the other jobs."

Thea stared at Jerry, wondering if the man was speaking Swahili. "Cell phone?" she asked, her tired mind latching on to the word that was most familiar. "Other jobs? What other jobs?"

Jerry groaned and drew a hand down his face. "Oh, sh— shoot. Didn't he tell you he was a contractor?"

"Tell me? Damon?" Thea said, sarcasm tainting her tone. "Do you have him mixed up with some sensitive nineties guy? Damon doesn't tell me anything." She thought about their conversation this morning. "Well, I guess he does a bit. But nothing about cell phones and job sites."

Jerry regarded the ceiling a moment. "Yeah, well, he's like that. Takes him awhile to open up, you know?"

"Awhile?"

"Actually, he's the most private person I've ever known." He turned to the door. "If you see him, tell him I'm looking for him, will you?"

Thea thought she'd used up every ounce of energy this morning, but when she saw Jerry reach for the screen-door handle, she realized she had a few deep reserves she could call on. Running toward him, she grabbed him by the back of the shirt. He was too polite to wrench free of her grasp.

"Jerry," she said grimly, "you accepted my offer of a cup of coffee. I'll make it a whole pot, or a six-pack, or whatever it takes. But I'm tired of this...crap." She almost smiled at the sound of such a word coming out of her mouth. Damon would be proud of her. "You come in the kitchen right now and tell me all about him...please?"

"I don't do that." Jerry faced her. "Talk about him, or his business especially. Like I said, he's a real private guy."

"Private?" Thea exclaimed. Didn't Jerry understand how much this meant to her? "Isn't it reasonable for me to ask for a little background on the man who's going to rebuild my house? On whom the success of my future business depends? My independence? The man I lo-l-l—" She managed to bite off the last word, but it took an effort.

Jerry's blue eyes smiled first, then his mouth. What started as a grin turned into a laugh. "No kidding?" he said. "You and Damon? Perfect. Damn, old Dora was right."

"No, Jerry," Thea said as primly as she could. "Not me and Damon. I said nothing about Damon, who has made it perfectly clear that he doesn't even like being around me. He feels obligated simply because of Auntie."

"Oh, yeah," Jerry said. "I noticed that down at the job

site, that he don't feel a thing except obligation to your aunt.''

"What *are* you talking about?"

"I saw the way he looked at you," Jerry said, his grin broad. "It sure as hell wasn't obligation I saw in his eyes."

Embarrassed, Thea looked away. Jerry was surely confusing desire, which neither she nor Damon could deny, with deeper feelings.

"Let's stick to the point, Jerry. Right now, Damon's business is my business. I need to know everything I can about him so I can get my variance." She gestured toward the kitchen. "You can tell me over lunch."

"I've got a sandwich back at—"

"I'm starving, so you might as well eat with me." She walked toward the kitchen as if she had no doubt Jerry would follow her.

He sat at the kitchen table while she scrubbed wallpaper gunk off her hands. She was glad she'd offered him lunch. If she kept puttering around the kitchen, Jerry probably wouldn't feel so much like he'd been roped into an inquisition. Just a couple of friends talking.

She stuck the remains of last night's turkey divan casserole into the oven to reheat and began cutting up vegetables for a salad. Or perhaps simply to keep her hands busy.

"Now tell me why Damon needs a cell phone and what are those other jobs you mentioned?" She hacked off the tip of her thumbnail as she let the chopping knife get too close. That was enough carrots anyway; she didn't really even like carrots in salad. "I thought you both worked for someone else, some contractor."

Jerry turned the mug around and around in his hands. "Damon's the contractor. He's building four houses this summer...well, actually three houses and a garage that's an add-on to a house he built last summer."

Thea put the knife down and leaned back against the counter, trying to assimilate the knowledge Jerry was giving her. "How many houses did he build last summer?"

"Three," Jerry said, "but one was really big. On the lake, seventy-six hundred square feet. Guy's from California, in movies or something."

Thea reached for a zucchini. "How...? What...?" She looked down and saw she'd sliced the whole squash. With a sigh, she put down the knife and began tearing up lettuce. "Half this town hates him, thinks he's a delinquent. I doubt Silas knows he's done an honest day's work in years. Now you tell me he's a very successful contractor. How can he hide something like that?"

"Human nature." Jerry chuckled. "What did you think of me when you met me on the street? The way I looked and all?"

Thea felt heat rush up her face to the roots of her hair. Oh, how she longed for a nice brunette complexion that didn't give away her feelings so easily. Thank heavens he couldn't see her face.

But Jerry obviously had no trouble reading her. "Go ahead. Tell the truth."

"Well, I guess it was mostly because of your motorcycle," Thea said. "And the ponytail. I assumed you were...uh..."

"A Hell's Angel?"

"Something like that." She put the salad plates on the table. "Of course, I thought you didn't have a job. Lounging around on the street that way in the middle of the day."

"Right." He gave her an open look. "Now what do you think?"

"That you're nothing like that," Thea said. "I mean, you're obviously hardworking and loyal." She grinned. "In fact, you seem, well, gentlemanly."

"So that's your answer," Jerry said. "The half of Pine

Butte that thinks of Damon as a rebel or a troublemaker sees him the way you saw me the other day.''

"But it's such a little town," Thea said. "Why doesn't everyone figure it out?"

"Little towns are notorious for gossip," Jerry said. "Like some guy who used to know him, a teacher or something, he'll see Damon on his bike, or coming out of a bar, and he'll think, there's that Free kid, never changes." He shrugged. "That's what he'll tell people."

"But what about all the people he works for?"

"Yeah," Jerry replied. "That's the half of town that thinks he's okay. First guy he built a house for here after he came back was his engineering prof from Cal Tech."

"Cal Tech!" Thea nearly dropped the casserole she was taking out of the oven. "How did he get into Cal Tech? And…I mean everyone thinks he just went away to start somewhere else and—"

"I know," Jerry agreed. "They think he came back because he failed in some other town. But he really came back to take care of your aunt."

"I know. But…?"

"I can't believe Damon didn't tell you this stuff." Jerry shook his head. "Actually I can. He never talks about himself. Never lies, just lets people draw their own conclusions." He turned up a palm. "Thinks it's a big joke."

"I'm really laughing," Thea grumbled. "Tell me about Cal Tech."

Jerry shrugged. "Dora got him in. She had an old friend there, a full professor. Deal was, if he didn't get top grades first semester, he was out. He got a four point…every year. Degree in construction engineering." He avoided her eyes by spooning turkey divan onto his plate. "Dora paid his tuition, too. I guess you could figure that."

"Take it all, Jerry," Thea said, gesturing at the casserole.

"I couldn't eat a thing." She picked up her coffee. "So was that Dora's friend who wanted the house built?"

"Yeah," Jerry said between bites. "This is good."

"Thanks, keep talking."

"The guy wanted a summer home up here. He liked it, told his friends what a great job Damon did." He forked salad. "But his friends were from California, too."

"What about the woman at the lumberyard?" Thea asked, her mind reeling. "And the subcontractors he works with?"

"A town like this, with all these summer people," Jerry said, "kind of has two cultures. Sure, some out-of-stater buys land, asks Marsha who's a good builder, she'll tell him Damon. But someone who's always lived here, he won't ask Marsha. He already has an opinion of Damon. Marsha can't change it." He gave a mirthless chuckle. "Who's the best contractor in town is not a hot topic of conversation—except for people about to build a house."

"But that's so silly," Thea said. "Damon could dispel their bad opinion easily."

"You mean like join the chamber of commerce or something?"

"Things like that, yes."

"Yeah, he could," Jerry said. "And I kind of think he would have, except when he came home after college, everyone he saw—except Dora and Roni—they acted like, hey, what're you doing back, like…" He frowned, searching for the word.

Thea wanted to cry. "Like he didn't belong in his own hometown."

Jerry shot her a grateful look. "Yeah, exactly. So I guess he just figured, I'll show them. This is his way of proving how wrong and blind they are. Wants to be the first rebel millionaire biker or something." He reached for the serving spoon and took another helping. "I'll tell you something else, what I started to tell you the other day. Damon hired me when no one else would. Lot of the guys who work for him are like that."

"Why couldn't you get a job?" Thea asked. "I've seen you work. Don't tell me it's *your* motorcycle image."

A grin tilted Jerry's lips. "Nah. When I was a marine, I got in a fight in the enlisted men's club. More like a brawl. About seventy of us got kicked out of the service with a general discharge instead of an honorable. You try to find work after that." His knuckles turned white around his fork and he jabbed it viciously into a piece of turkey. "One damn fight, and I'm supposed to be out of work the rest of my life."

"Damon isn't stupid," Thea said. "He could see that you—"

"Nah, he couldn't," Jerry interrupted. "No one could. I came home, couldn't even get work here. I started drinking. My wife was supporting us. Damon took a chance is what he did."

Wife? Thea thought. "Does he ever take chances on people who don't work out?"

"Sure, sometimes, but not often," Jerry said. "He's a good judge of character. But you got to figure, guys like me who work for him, well, we're damn loyal. So, okay, I may think this privacy thing…well, maybe it's not the way I'd go. But if he wants to hide behind a leather jacket, it's all right with me."

"But it's only making him hurt more," Thea protested. "He could make his life much more comfortable if he'd just get the chip off his shoulder."

"Maybe." Jerry shrugged. "But it's a damn big chip. Take someone or something bigger'n me to knock it off. I ain't gonna try." He pushed his chair back from the table. "Will you give my wife the recipe for that?"

"Of course," Thea said, wondering how she could talk

about things so mundane when her head was spinning from everything Jerry had told her. "My phone number's the same as Dora's."

He stood. "I'd better get back to work. I'll ask Darlene to call you."

"Darlene?"

"Yeah, my wife."

Jerry's wife? Darlene was Jerry's wife? Thea took a deep breath. "Does Darlene have long blond hair and... sparkly eyes?"

Jerry grinned proudly. "Yeah, sparkly eyes. That's a good description. Did you meet her somewhere?"

"I just saw her downtown one day...on Damon's motorcycle."

Jerry nodded. "Must have been that day she had a flat."

"How do you know?"

"She never gets on Damon's bike unless she has to," Jerry said. "Scares her to ride without a sissy bar."

"Me, too," Thea said. "That's why you have to scrunch up close and hang on."

Jerry's grin turned to a look of male possession. "You, maybe. Darlene only rides that way with me." He turned to leave. "If you see Damon, tell him I'm looking for him, will you?"

For once, Thea didn't walk a guest to the door. She wasn't sure her knees would function all the way down the hall.

CHAPTER NINE

WHEN Thea thought her legs would support her, she straightened the kitchen and went back to wallpaper removal. Within a few minutes, she was cursing the man—surely it was a man—who had invented the wallpaper steamer. But she didn't stop.

Mindless as the motions of wallpaper steaming were, they had become so exhausting, it took most of her concentration to keep working. But even with just a tiny part of her brain dwelling on all she'd learned about Damon the past few days, Thea reeled. Why had he lied to her?

Well, that wasn't exactly right. Damon hadn't lied, ever. As Jerry had said, Damon was an open book—to anyone who bothered to look. Thea had made snap judgments about him, from his long hair, his record, his—she had to admit it—his motorcycle. She'd never bothered to look beneath the surface. And Damon had gladly let her keep that wrong impression.

So had Dora, Thea realized with a start. At least she'd never said anything, nor left *her* a letter, to dispel Thea's...prejudice. Was this Auntie's last lesson? Her final reminder to forget appearances and look for the real beauty underneath.

With a groan, Thea dropped the steamer, wondering if she'd ever have the strength in her arms to pick it up again. She staggered downstairs, slumped into a chair at the kitchen table and leaned her head on her folded arms.

As she let herself think of Damon without distractions, she realized that, from the beginning, it had only been her strictly trained intellect that had judged Damon falsely. She cringed inwardly, knowing she'd acted just like the residents of Pine Butte who'd judged him unfairly most of his life.

She had never listened to her body. Since the first time he kissed her at seventeen, her body had known—and had reminded her every time another man touched her—that Damon was the only man for her.

And her heart knew, though it had wisely waited for a little more evidence than mere desire before it overwhelmed Thea with the knowledge that she loved him. Would always love him. Had never loved another.

But her mind had absorbed Father and Chelsea's fear of the Prebble flaw, that dreaded wild streak of her mother's, and made Thea afraid to believe in her feelings for Damon. Had, in fact, convinced her that all she felt was lust. If Damon's hair were blond, she wondered, his eyes blue, would she have figured out her true feelings earlier?

Thea yawned, unmoved by a vision of Damon with blue eyes. She did love him, she wanted to commit herself to him forever. But she *was* still a Prebble, and his dark eyes and black hair, his olive skin... Thea quivered and let her eyelids flutter shut.

A nagging question about Damon drifted around her sleepy brain, just out of grasp of her consciousness. A bit of the picture that didn't fit. Maybe she'd think of it as she slept, for surely she would dream about Damon.

Thea felt warmth near her cheek and blinked. Someone had turned on the kitchen lights, so night must have fallen. She yawned deeply and the aroma of fried chicken hit her, reminding her she'd eaten no lunch.

She lifted her head. "Damon?" she murmured, fighting off sleep.

"I brought dinner," Damon said, gesturing at the box of chicken on the table. "Jerry told me how hard you were

working.'' He snorted. "Then I come in and find you napping on the job.''

"Napping." Thea closed her eyes again. The fuzzy end
of her dream flitted through her mind and she remembered
what it was she needed to ask Damon. "This was more
serious than a nap, Damon. I was exhausted." She sat up,
arching her back and stretching her arms. "Ooo, I'm sore."

Damon shook his head in mock dismay. "Whining about
the work already?''

He stepped behind her chair and began to massage her
upper arms. Thea felt as if she would melt into her chair.

"Oh, that feels good." She sighed.

Damon's hands moved to the back of her neck, his
thumbs making circles between her shoulder blades, and
Thea could barely make her lips form words.

"Damon," she said, without opening her eyes.

"Yeah?"

"You and Auntie were really good friends."

"The best."

"So you told her everything?"

Damon chuckled and Thea felt it come down his arms
into his fingers and onto her flesh. "Not *everything*,
Prebble. A man needs a little privacy. But everything that
mattered.''

Thea kept her voice light. "Then I guess she knew you
weren't really Matt's father?"

"Yeah," Damon said. "Dora knew all ab—"

His hands froze on her back, his thumbs pressing hard
into the muscles along her spine. Thea twisted away from
the painful pressure.

"You sneaky, underhanded, devious—" He cut off his
words with a furious oath.

"It wasn't really hard to figure out, Damon."

Thea stood and turned to face him. Damon backed up a
step, as if touching her had become repellent to him.

"Yesterday you tell me you're going to restore my house for nothing just because you gave your word to someone who's dead, and then you expect me to believe you'd abandon a child you'd fathered?" She stretched a palm toward his cheek, but he jerked his head away. "I'm not a fool, Damon."

He drew his hand down his face. "You have no idea what you're talking about. Nor the damage you can do."

"I think I figured it out because of the wallpaper," she reflected.

"Ri-ight. The wallpaper. That makes a lot of sense."

"You're the wall, Damon, hidden under all those layers of covering." She followed his movements with her eyes only as he began to pace the kitchen, afraid to spook him further. "I just got through all the layers in some places, and I liked what I saw beneath."

"You've been cute enough tonight, Thea," Damon growled. "Don't try it anymore. It's a real pain in the ass."

He strode out of the kitchen.

Thea winced at the sound of the front door slamming. Without his energizing presence, she could think only of her aching arms. Probably she had been too "cute". But Damon had let his guard down. He thought she was still half-asleep while he was wide-awake.

The door slammed again and Damon's footsteps came heavily back down the hall toward her. Thea tensed, gladly. Jerking a chair out from under the table, Damon spun it around and straddled it.

Frustration etched his face and his voice came out full of anger. "I guess I should have just lied. But I didn't figure you for the kind of female who would trick me into saying something I didn't want to."

Thea folded her hands in front of her on the table to keep herself from trying to touch him. "I think it's more because you think your leather-jacket reputation hides your true nature.''

Damon snorted. "You don't know anything about me."

Thea pursed her lips. "More than you'd think, Damon. I know you're a lot madder at yourself right now than at me."

"Damn right!" he exploded. "I gave my word!"

"I can understand why that bothers you," Thea said. "Of course, I hope you're going to explain this strange lie to me, because it doesn't make much sense. But if you're worried that I'll say something to someone, you don't need to. I learned that from both Dora and Father."

"Dora and your old man agreed on something?"

Thea smiled. "On what it means to give one's word? They agreed completely, though I'm sure they never discussed it. And they didn't phrase it exactly the same way." She pushed back a straggly curl covered with wallpaper glue and looked straight at Damon. "I give you my word, Damon, I'll never tell anyone anything you've told me. About this or any other subject you ask me to keep secret. I'm not a blabbermouth."

He looked at her a long time, minutes. Thea was squirming when he finally expelled a gusty breath. "I'll tell you. I've got to so you'll understand why it can't ever go any further." He stood. "But not because I trust you, Prebble. I know better than that."

Thea's heart stuttered in pain at his words. He obviously hadn't wasted any of his precious time trying to figure her out, the way she had with him. Of course, she'd thought of almost nothing but Damon Free for days. He was probably thinking of Roni and Marsha and…who knew how many others.

"You can, though, Damon," she insisted. "No matter what you think."

"Ri-ight. Trust a woman."

"You trusted Dora."

He made a disrespectful noise. "*She* earned it. You've got a long way to go."

"Fine," Thea said, not troubling to hide the hurt in her voice. "Then don't tell me."

Damon swore again. "I wish I didn't have to." He dragged a hand through his hair, pulling tangled strands from his ponytail. "You don't understand little towns. When Roni told Mel she was pregnant, he already hated me. But so did most of Pine Butte."

"Hate? You don't—"

He waved her to silence. "Maybe that's too strong. They'd written me off, that's for damn sure. Mel wasn't the only father who didn't want his daughter anywhere near me. But he caught her one night sneaking in after a date with me. So it wasn't surprising that he figured it was all my fault, that I'd seduced Roni, that she was blameless."

"Right," Thea said. "I do understand that. What I don't underst—"

This time, Damon used a ferocious glare to stifle her words. "I know…Matt's real father." Damon picked up a fork from beside his plate and began stabbing it through the side of the fried-chicken box. "When Roni was a kid, there was this guy, a friend of her father's, who she used to see all the time. In fact, the two families, his and Mel's, were friends. They socialized a lot. In high school, when she was having all those normal adolescent problems, she talked to him about stuff and he was very understanding."

"Like Dora and you."

"No!" Damon said. The steam coming from the holes he was making caught his attention, and he transferred his ire to the paper napkins. "No one was like Dora. But he was pretty good at it, trained for it, actually. Roni began to believe she was in love with him, and she was old enough to act on it, eighteen. She was so beautiful, so loving, and he'd known her for so long...I guess he just couldn't resist her. Once."

"Once." Thea shook her head. "But why didn't she tell her father?"

"Can't you see what that would do?" he asked, exasperated. "The whole town would know. This guy was, still is, Mel's best friend. Roni's mom and his wife are friends. The families have Christmas dinner together. Then and now. With this guy's other kids and his grandkids. And Matt." Damon met her gaze with a ferocious glare. "Besides, he's the minister of their church."

"The minister?" Thea exclaimed. "No wonder she talked to him about her problems." She groaned. "I guess the truth would tear up more than their families."

With an obvious effort, Damon put the fork down and scooped the napkin shreds into the palm of his hand. "Now you see. It would mess up the whole community, at least for a while. But if she let Mel think it was me...hell, no one would be surprised. She just never said anything to anyone. Not even to Mel. He drew his own conclusions." He stood to throw the shreds into the wastebasket under the sink.

"But why did you go along with it?"

"Hey, why should I care? I was about to leave, and I figured I'd never be coming back. If anyone else thought the same thing as Mel, well, I was used to it by then." He shrugged that tight shrug that Thea had learned meant he was filled with tension. "Roni was one of my few good friends—she asked me not to say anything, so I didn't."

"But then you did decide to come back to Pine Butte, Damon, and—"

"Actually," he interrupted, "I began to realize before I moved back, when I came to visit Dora, that things were getting kind of mixed up this way." He faced her and leaned back against the counter. "But I promised Roni. It's her decision what to say, when to say it, who to say it to."

"What about Matt?" Thea asked. "What does Roni tell him?"

"Yeah, that's the bad part," Damon agreed. His voice softened when he spoke of Matt; in fact his whole body seemed more relaxed. "Roni and I've talked about it. She tells Matt that when he's old enough, she'll explain to him about his father."

Thea tried not to sound judgmental. "What does he think of you?"

Damon's eyes flitted around the kitchen as if he couldn't bring himself to meet her eyes. "That's a problem. I really like the kid." He turned up his palms. "I take him to school every day on my bike—he loves it. I try not to go to all his Little League games, but I kind of can't help it. I love to watch him play."

Thea felt her eyes start to fill with tears she had no intention of shedding. She feared doing *anything* that might discourage Damon from talking this way and revealing so much about himself. How could Damon's kind heart remain invisible to so many people in Pine Butte?

"I tell him the truth, though," Damon said defensively. "'Course I'm not sure what he believes." He winced. "I tell him I'm not his father, that I wish I were."

He let his gaze rest on her face; warmth made his charcoal eyes glow as if they were on fire. Thea longed to take him in her arms, but she didn't move.

"I was here when Roni had the baby. It was..." An expression of intense emotion crossed Damon's face. "Have you ever seen a baby born?"

Thea had a sudden vivid image of herself having Damon's baby, so powerful she could barely get an answer out. "No."

"Hard to believe what it does to you."

"*Mel* let you in the delivery room?" Thea asked, stunned. "Didn't the whole town know?"

"Mel's a jerk," Damon said. "But he loves his daughter. He wouldn't deny her something when she's in pain. Besides, no one knew. She wasn't in town."

"Why not?"

"She had some trouble early and they took her to Billings. She asked a nurse to call me." He smiled. "It was 2:00 a.m. and damn cold. It's about a three-hour drive. I'm on my bike, freezing, thinking I'm nuts to do this. But it was worth it."

Damon looked distractedly around the kitchen, his gaze lighting on the chair. He sat on it sideways, his long, jeans-clad legs sticking out. "Something about the kid turning out to be a boy...got to me. I just couldn't see letting him grow up without any man the right age acting interested. Like I knew his father wasn't ever going to come forward. Mel loves him, but he's a granddad, and I—" He pulled his hand down his face.

Thea could tell he wasn't going to say any more. "You amaze me, Damon. What would the townspeople think if they knew you were fathering a boy not your own?"

In one swift movement, Damon rose from his chair and leaned over hers, grabbing her arm with one hand and her chin with the other. His angry gaze made her feel like a bird under scrutiny by a cat. "I don't know. I'll never know. Because they are never going to find out. Except from Roni. Not from you."

"Of course not, Damon," Thea said indignantly. "I gave you my word."

"I wish I could believe it." He released her and turned toward the door. As he passed the table, he gestured at the containers from the store. "Help yourself, Prebble. I'm not hungry anymore."

Thea trotted down the hall after him, though she knew

it was a waste of time. He didn't stop at the door, barely slowed down to get his bike started. She stood in the square of light, listening to the roar of his machine disappear up the hill.

Too soon, silence descended. She returned to the kitchen to put away the untouched food.

For the first time, she noticed that Damon had put wine-glasses beside their plates on the table. When she opened the refrigerator, she found a bottle of white wine and one of soda water.

Tears she'd fought for an hour filled her eyes again, making her vision blurry. Damon had brought her the makings of a spritzer. Jerry must have told him she liked them.

The tenderness of the gesture made her heart ache with joy and anguish. He'd brought her a spritzer, and she'd turned him away with questions that were none of her business.

Thea reached for the bottle of wine, deciding she wouldn't bother with soda tonight. It would water down the numbing qualities of the wine she wanted. But as her fingers closed around the icy neck of the bottle, she changed her mind.

She didn't want to drink Damon's wine without Damon. Loving this man—this kindhearted, pigheaded man—was going to frustrate her as long as she knew him. But she wouldn't let him drive her to drink.

At the insistence of her muscles, Thea took the next afternoon off. Besides, she had just a week left to prepare her arguments for the city council meeting. If she showed up with nothing more than sore arms and a belief in the town's injustice to Damon, she wouldn't accomplish anything.

Two of the state's daily newspapers had agreed to cover the meeting. It wasn't exactly like having CNN show up, but it would certainly make the city council listen to Thea's arguments. She hoped.

Over a cup of cold coffee, Thea reread the list of council members she'd gotten from the city clerk. The only name she recognized was Mel's. She needed to learn who these people were, whether any of the rest of them carried grudges against Damon, who would be easiest to persuade.

As Thea showered off wallpaper gunk, she thought of the things Jerry had told her. She wished she could slip down to the lake for another conversation with him, perhaps with her list of councilmen in hand. But as Damon felt so strongly about privacy, it didn't seem right to ask Jerry to discuss his boss at work.

Glancing in the mirror, she noticed the brunette rinse was washing out of her hair. A beauty parlor might be a good place to get some local gossip; it usually was. But that wasn't the sort of gossip she wanted. She might hear about Damon's love life there, but not his work life.

Besides, she planned to commit every penny she had to this restoration. That meant giving up hair salons for the duration of the summer. If her hair grew back to the carroty red that Chelsea found so common, she'd just have to live with it.

She dressed, pulled her hair into two ponytails, hoping to keep most of it from escaping, and drove to the lumberyard. What a stroke of good fortune that this business, the center of the building industry in Pine Butte, was run by a woman.

When Thea arrived, the woman who must be Marsha was talking rapidly to three customers at once, somehow managing to keep their questions and their orders separate. She had frizzy, dark brown hair with a dyed purple streak over her right eye, long-fingered hands that never held still and a deep but very female voice. Moreover, she obviously had an enormous knowledge of her business.

Thea waited until the men left before approaching her.
"Are you Marsha?"

"Yeah," the woman said, not friendly, not rude. "What
can I do for you?"

"I'd like to talk to you," Thea said. "About Damon
Free."

Marsha ran her gaze over Thea. "You Thea Birch?" she
asked. "Dora's niece?"

"Yes. Can we talk in private?"

Marsha looked around the building and rolled her eyes.
"Private?"

"Don't you have an office?"

"Yeah, but it's about as private as Grand Central
Station," Marsha said. "Door hasn't been closed in ten
years. I don't think the hinges work anymore." She
laughed. "Great ad for the lumber business, right?"

"Can I buy you lunch?" Thea glanced at the clock over
the counter and saw it was nearly two. "Or maybe dinner
tonight? Do you already have plans?"

"Anyone with five kids *always* has plans," Marsha told
her. "Let's go now." She said something to the high-
school boy behind the counter and walked out with Thea
without even grabbing her purse. "Let's get out of here
quick, before someone else needs me." In Thea's car,
Marsha pulled a pack of cigarettes out of her shirt pocket.
"Mind if I smoke up your car?"

Thea did, but she didn't say so.

Marsha lit one and took a drag. "Damon said you're
going ahead with this B&B thing, even though the variance
guys turned you down."

"That's right."

"Well, I'm always ready for a good fight," Marsha said,
sounding leery. "But I hate to see Damon get sucked into
it. He spent enough years fighting everyone in this town.
You think maybe what you're doing will hurt him?"

Thea pursed her lips in irritation. "I think Damon is doing more to hurt himself than I can do. He's such a... a...blockhead!"

Marsha was smiling now. "The word you're looking for is *stubborn ass*. But, hey, he's a man. They look at things a different way."

"The wrong way," Thea sniffed.

"Yeah, probably," Marsha said. "The motel out on the highway's the best place if you want private. No one there but tourists."

Thea started the car and drove toward the motel. "In your business, don't you work almost entirely with men? That must be hard sometimes."

"No." Marsha laughed. "It's hard all the time."

At the restaurant, after they'd ordered fajitas and the waitress had left, Thea pulled out the list of councilmen. "I don't know any of these people," she said. "Except that awful Mel. Do any of the others hate Damon as much?"

Marsha barely glanced at the list. She poked at one name with the hand that held her cigarette, leaving behind a small burn on the page. "That guy, Bill, he's the vice-principal of the high school and was when Damon attended. The vice-principal's in charge of discipline. He probably thinks less of Damon than anyone in town."

"Less than Mel?"

Marsha wobbled her hand back and forth to indicate that was a toss-up. "This woman here—" she pointed at another name "—Katey, she doesn't really have anything against him, but she's the worst gossip in the state. She's been on the council about three years, listening to Mel and Bill. She believes the worst."

"What makes you think they'd bother to turn her against him?" Thea asked. "Why would his name come up at all?"

"She and her husband built an addition to their house a

couple of years ago. I told her she ought to let Damon do it.'' Marsha quieted a moment while the waitress put their plates in front of them and filled their coffee cups. ''I thought it'd be good for Damon to do a house for one of the townies. Katey laughed in my face.''

''It's so *infuriating*!'' Thea splatted sour cream on top of peppers and onions. ''Damon said I ought to fire him, then reapply.''

''You'd get your variance like that.'' Marsha snapped her fingers, scattering ashes. ''You gonna do that?''

''Not on your life!''

''Good,'' Marsha said, rolling her tortilla. ''I'll tell you something. Damon Free is the best customer I have. He bargains hard, I admit. But he gets things done when he says, which is good for my reputation, too. He backs his work. He pays on time or early. Every damn penny. The subs like working for him because he pays them on time, too. If there's trouble getting paid by the customer, Damon's the one who fights the battle. He's the one who eats the loss.'' She wiped her hands on her napkin so she could gesture effectively. ''He's the most ethical man I've ever known.''

''Then why…?''

Marsha rolled her eyes. ''Dumb, huh? That's why I called him a stubborn ass. He thinks it's funny that everyone he works with thinks he's a damn pillar of society, and everyone who doesn't thinks he's a disreputable pot-smoking, bike-riding miscreant.''

Thea watched Marsha light another cigarette and thought about what she meant to do. ''Marsha, my house was the first ever built in Pine Butte. No one would want it torn down, would they? Not even the people on the council.''

''Of course not. They're all for local history.'' She exhaled slowly. ''Anyone who's thought about it knows you can't afford to fix the old place up unless you're going to make money off it. What they don't know is what a great job Damon would do restoring it. Personally, there's not another builder in this town I'd trust with the job. If you don't hire Damon, you'll have to go out of town.''

''Wouldn't that mean the subs would come from out of town, too?''

''It might,'' Marsha conceded.

''Isn't that something the council would want to avoid?'' Thea insisted. ''Driving all that business out of town?''

''They *should*,'' Marsha said dubiously.

''Will you come tell the city council what you told me? Publicly?''

Marsha exhaled through her nostrils. ''If I have to.''

''I think you'd want to!'' Thea exclaimed. ''After what you said about Damon. Will you give me the names of the subs who work with him, people he's built houses for? So I can—''

''I'll do it if you really want,'' Marsha said. ''And I'll come to the meeting and say whatever you want. But you'd better think about it, sweetie, because when Damon hears what you plan to do, he's going to go ballistic.''

CHAPTER TEN

THEA sat in Auntie's window seat, watching streaks of red from the setting sun move across the lake. Her thoughts turned to all she'd learned about Damon this week. Almost everyone she'd talked to had agreed with what Marsha had told her about Damon's work and character.

Not that they all liked him; some found his leather-jacketed facade not only foolish but annoying. Even so, they still said they wouldn't hire anyone else to build a house.

Unfortunately, they *all* agreed with Marsha about one thing: Damon would surely "go ballistic" at the meeting. However, most said they'd come anyway, and those who liked him agreed to speak.

None of that bothered Thea. She hadn't a doubt in her mind she was doing the right thing as far as Damon was concerned. The dilemma she faced tonight was one of the heart.

Why had she waited to tell Damon she loved him? She should have told him the moment she knew it, and damn the consequences! That's the sort of love Damon would respect.

Instead, she'd let her fears of the Prebble flaw, of not following Chelsea's rules of propriety, her pride, keep her from telling him how much she loved him before she knew he returned her feelings. Even when she knew that no matter what his feelings for her she would still love him till the day she died, she'd remained silent. Afraid.

And *now* what could she say? Darling Damon, the more

I learn about your successful business, the more I love you? However she phrased it, he would regard it with suspicion.

The sound of a motorcycle drew her gaze up the hill to the top of her drive. Thea couldn't say exactly how she knew he was angry just from watching him ride toward her. But she did. He drove faster, spinning out when he made the curves, winding out in each gear till the motor screamed.

When he dismounted and strode toward the door, anger showed in every line of his body. Thea's stomach knotted tightly. She had a good idea what had infuriated him.

As his boots stomped across the porch, Thea suddenly knew her bedroom wasn't the right place to discuss anything with Damon in his current mood. She ran down the stairs to the sound of his fist pounding against the door.

She reached for the door just as Damon shoved it open. "Damon, what—"

"What the hell do you think you're up to," he demanded without preamble, "prying into my business?"

Thea closed her eyes a moment, gathering her resolve. "I wouldn't call it prying, Damon. After all, it's my business, too. I mean, it will be if I get this variance."

"Like hell it's not prying," he said. "What if I called that prig your father wants you to marry and asked him all about you? Would you call that prying?"

"That's not the same thing at all," Thea said. "I didn't call your many girlfriends, Damon. I only chatted with—"

"How do you know how many girlfriends I have?" he demanded.

"Well, of course, I don't," she conceded. "I just... assumed..." Heat rushed into her cheeks.

Damon grabbed her arm and pulled her into the unused formal front parlor. Though Thea had removed the dust sheets from the furniture, she'd done little else in here, and the room felt uninhabited. Heavy velvet drapes shrouded soot-darkened windows, leaving the room dim and chilly.

Damon tugged her to a Queen Anne chair so faded the original color was a mystery. Thea sat, but Damon remained on his feet above her, making her feel as if she'd already lost the argument.

"Damon, your girlfriends are beside the point. I want to run a business. I need a variance, and the reputation of my contractor is a factor in whether I get one. I've done nothing except prepare my arguments to present to the city council."

"Argue about yourself, Prebble," he said. "Leave me out of it."

"You know I can't," Thea said. "Not and win."

Damon grabbed her arms and pulled her up toward him. His eyes sparked with fury. "Butt out, Prebble. You don't understand. You never will."

Thea closed her eyes; she couldn't think staring at him. "What don't I understand?" She raised her lids. "I know you as well as Dora did."

"Not even close." He dropped her back on the age-flattened cushion. "We're outcasts, Dora and I. You're not, never have been. You follow the rules."

Thea opened her mouth to protest, but no words came out. She couldn't argue; he was right. She'd never rebelled, not truly. Even starting this B&B against Father's wishes, she was staying within the structure Damon rejected. In it, she found the comfort he still sought. She wanted to make him see that.

She stood and took his face between her palms. "Tomorrow night, when all your friends speak for you—"

He put his hands on the arm of her chair. "No one will speak for me." His voice was cold and final.

"Why not?" Thea cried. "You can't go on like this. It's

not fair to you.'' A cool breeze from the hallway sent shivers down her arms.

"If you think I'm going to go before those 'pillars' of the community and grovel that way, you're out of your mind." He glared at the empty fireplace, a muscle jumping in his cheek. "If they really did their jobs right, they'd already know everything you can tell them. They certainly ought to know it before they vote on your variance application." His voice rose. "Shouldn't they?"

"Well, of course they should, Damon," Thea answered. "But no one's perfect. This is a little town. They think they already know. But this isn't about them, it's about you."

"You're not going to do it, Thea," Damon said adamantly. "It's too much like begging, like asking forgiveness for my past sins, when I don't believe I sinned all that damned much."

"You didn't sin at all, Damon," Thea said. "You were a child. They're the ones who failed. They could have helped you and they didn't. After tomorrow night, they'll see that. They'll see that you made it on your own, with no help from any of them, just from one great old lady." She put a hand on his chest to push him back from her. "They'll ask *your* forgiveness if it means so darn much to you!"

"They won't, because they won't hear any of this." He wasn't angry now, wasn't arguing. He was simply issuing an edict.

But it was a foolish, stubborn-male-ego sort of edict! Thea wanted to cry. Not for her, not even for her variance. For Damon—he was the one keeping himself an outcast. Because he was an obstinate male with too much pride to be reasonable. The way a woman would be.

The way Thea would be. If it was about her. But this was about Damon.

He must be reading her thoughts. "Thea Birch, you gave

me your word you wouldn't ever blab something I asked you to keep private."

"I said I'd keep secret anything you told me, Damon. But you didn't tell me any of this. I found it out for myself." The sun slid behind the mountains, darkening the light that spilled in from the hallway. Shadows filled every corner of the room, and the pine-scented breeze turned cool. Thea shivered and rubbed her arms. "Not that it was hard to discover. You're not a secret agent or anything."

"Exactly my point," Damon said. "Anyone who wants to know about me can figure it out for himself. You will not enlighten them."

He glared at her hands moving up and down her arms. Pulling off his black sweatshirt, he tugged it over her head. It tumbled down her body, covering her in his heat nearly to her knees. As his intensely male scent—a mixture of sweat and soap and fresh-cut wood and dust from the road—rose around her, she couldn't help the small sigh of comfort that escaped her.

"You're making a mistake, Damon," she told him.

"It's my mistake to make."

Thea's shoulders slumped. She felt as if they slumped down to her toes. "It's mine, too, Damon. What about my variance?"

"You'll have to win a different way." The look he gave her was so filled with anger, he probably thought he was hiding the hurt Thea found just as easy to recognize. "If that's all you care about, I'm sure you'll find another tactic."

"Of course it's not all I care about, you pighead!" She reached for Damon with a hand covered by the long sleeve of his shirt. "I don't want you...to feel like this anymore. It's too painful. You don't deserve it."

Damon took both her hands in his. "I thought you were different, Prebble." The pain in his voice hurt her like a slap across the face. "I thought you understood about living free, breaking loose." He shook his head. "But now... It's like now you've discovered how acceptable I am, you can hardly wait to clean me up for Father and Chelsea."

"Oh, Damon!" Thea would have slapped him if she could have gotten a hand free. He must have realized it because he tightened his grip on her fingers. "Don't you understand anything? I love you! I'll tell Father and Chelsea that, I'll tell the city council, I'll tell the whole world. And the only one who won't believe me is *you!*"

Damon stared. In his surprise, he released her hands and Thea fled the room.

Chasing after her, Damon caught her with her foot on the bottom stair. Spinning her around, he crushed her between the wall and his body.

"Prebble, I..." For once, for just a second, Damon sounded hesitant. Then he made that utterly male noise of his and covered her mouth with his.

Confidence rapidly replaced hesitation in every inch of his body. He didn't ask; he knew he didn't need to. For though he demanded, he asked nothing from her she did not long to give.

She held nothing back. Her body spoke for her. Whimpering and arching toward him, she let him know how much she craved his touch, how much she loved him.

"Damon, please," she moaned. "Please. Take me upstairs."

He pulled her close, holding her hard to him. "I can't. Not tonight."

"Can't?" Her mind struggled to make sense of his words.

"It's not enough, Prebble. I need more."

"More?" she whispered, close to tears. "I just told you I love you, and you need *more?*"

"I can't help it." He stroked her back, calming her.

"Trust matters more to me than anything. I can't know, not really, not until tomorrow night. I *have* to know that about you. Try to understand. I don't want it—I *need* it."

"Damon, how can you doubt me?"

He drew back and looked into her eyes. "I have to be sure." A slow smile started at his lips and spread across his face. "What's one more night? You've waited years." He put a palm on her bottom and slid it slowly up her spine to the back of her neck, cupping her head. "Though why in hell it's me you've waited for, I'll never understand."

"How do you know I waited?" she asked.

Damon nuzzled her beneath the ear. "Something's different," he murmured. "I can't explain it." He drew back and looked her in the eye. "Am I wrong?"

Thea blushed furiously and lowered her gaze. "None of your business." She hooked her fingers through his belt loops, holding him to her. "Do you feel different, too, Damon?"

"Goddamn right," he growled. He cupped her chin, letting his thumb softly caress her cheek. "You want to know how it feels for me? It hurts when I let you go. Around you, I hurt almost all the time."

The muscles in her face were melting at his touch. "You probably deserve it, Damon."

"I don't doubt it."

He kissed her again, deeply, making her ache with wanting. But when he let her go, she understood. She leaned against the wall of the house, watching him drive away on his motorcycle. Damon had been betrayed too many times in his life to trust blindly. He needed proof.

Oh, if only she hadn't waited to tell Damon she loved him!

The next evening, Thea waited for Damon on the porch, wishing the sight of the mountains could soothe her tonight as much as they had always calmed Dora. She had spent the day phoning as many as she could of the people she'd asked to the meeting to warn them she probably wouldn't ask them to speak. Most said they planned to come anyway.

She wondered if a fistfight would break out when the council denied her variance.

An hour ago, Damon had phoned with her first test of the evening—did she want to arrive at the meeting with him? Or had she decided that might be impolitic. Of *course* she did, Thea insisted, even if he wore one of his black tank tops.

So now she waited in anything but peace—her mind was in turmoil and at war with her heart. Should she go to the meeting and give Damon what he asked, begged for, in fact—proof that he could trust her? Even though doing so would certainly mean she'd lose her variance?

Or should she fail him, let him down, tell the world exactly what kind of a wonderful man he was—force him into the middle-class respectability he thought he despised?

She knew—as surely as she knew her love for him would never die—that Damon would be happier there. It might take him a while, but ultimately he would find comfort in the regard of his hometown.

But Thea would lose him.

She knew that, too, had not a shred of doubt in her mind.

The roar of a motorcycle drew her gaze, and she looked up the road at the man she loved riding toward her in the sunlight. And she wondered which meant more to her. Damon's happiness? Or her own?

Thea quit talking and gave the council members a few minutes to examine the stack of documents she'd given each of them. If she'd had any idea so many people would attend the meeting, she'd have made more copies.

Bill, the high-school vice-principal, looked up first. "Ms. Birch, you remind me a lot of your aunt." He gave her a genuine smile, the first she'd gotten from anyone on the council. "This is the way Dora would have done it, too. Overkill." He ruffled the pages she'd given him. "But you've convinced me. It'd be a damn shame to tear the old place down."

Thea's heart stuttered. It had been so easy. She smiled back, thinking of telling Damon, "I told you so," about the city council.

"Oh yes, Bill," said the councilwoman named Katey whom Marsha had warned her about. "It would be a great loss to our community."

Bill nodded and looked at the others. "Do we all agree? We overturn the variance committee's recommendation this time?"

The other council members were nodding when the mayor—a tall, thin man with practically no chin—spoke up at last. "Before we put this to a vote, I believe Mel has something to say."

Five heads turned to Mel. Thea's stomach lurched at the deference the other members seemed to give him.

"The only problem the committee had with this," Mel said, "is how we can best preserve this Pine Butte landmark." He shot Thea one of the coldest smiles she'd ever seen. "Now, I understand that the cost of restoring the structure would be prohibitive for you, Ms. Birch, unless you can make some money off it when it's done."

"Well, of course, Mel," Katey said. "That's why she—"

Mel pushed a palm toward her. "I know, Katey. But that means we're not talking here about a bunch of simple repairs to a house. The contractor who takes on this job has to be...a specialist."

"Yes, that's important." Katey nodded. "Someone who specializes in restoring old buildings."

One of the other councilmen grumbled something affirmative under his breath, and Bill said, "Right. Exactly."

A shiver traveled down Thea's spine. She had a strange feeling this seemingly spontaneous conversation among the council members had been rehearsed.

Mel looked at Thea. "So I think we all agree, Ms. Birch, that we have no problem granting your application, if you agree as a condition of the variance to hire a contractor qualified in historical renovations. One with credentials *and* experience. This house of yours—" he tapped the pile of documents "—is too precious to our town to turn over to just any contractor."

The moment had arrived. Thea had not expected it to come so soon—nor so blatantly. It made her choice *so* conspicuous. Which made it that much harder.

The insincerity in Mel's tone gave Thea chills. His pretense of caring about her house fooled no one; she doubted it was meant to.

But she could return hypocrisy for hypocrisy. She could simply agree to have this limitation imposed on her variance. It would change nothing. If the city council challenged her when she kept Damon on, she could easily prove his qualifications for the job.

Few would ever hear about it. The question would never reach this sort of public forum again. Certainly the Helena and Bozeman newspapers would never send reporters again, not after the reasonable appearance the city council had feigned tonight.

Thea looked behind her at Damon, leaning against the back wall. With his usual black jeans and motorcycle boots, he was wearing, possibly for her benefit, a white shirt. But the effect was spoiled by the black leather jacket he wore over it.

He returned her look without a flicker of humor in his gaze. Challenge was there, a hint of mistrust. Thea knew she would never get another chance to prove herself to Damon if she failed him now.

But the overriding emotion she read in Damon's gaze, the one probably invisible to everyone but her and his few close friends, was hurt. Her heart ached to see it. Its intensity—here in this bastion of Pine Butte respectability—stunned her. So powerful an emotion, but worse, so unnecessary.

Praying that one day Damon would understand, she faced the front of the room again. "Yes, of course I'd agree to that, Councilman," she said. She stood up, not really to make her point more forcefully. Her fear of what she was about to do made her too anxious to stay in her chair. "In fact, I can tell you already whom I plan to hire." She turned and pointed at him. "Mr. Damon Free."

"Damon Free!" Mel exploded, making no effort to keep his voice below a shout. "What the hell makes you think that degenerate's qualified to restore an old house—"

"Now, Mel," Katey interrupted. "We don't want to use that sort of language—" she nodded at the reporters "—*on the record*."

"We all know what that man's good for," Mel said, jabbing his finger furiously in Damon's direction, "and it ain't restorations! Probably tried it on Ms. Birch here, and that's why she wants him for her contractor."

Thea heard a growling noise come from Damon, not a loud one, but definitely not the kind he made when he had his arms around her. She spun to look at him, startled to see the rage on his face. A second later, he erased it, sliding back into his defiant shell.

Without straightening away from the wall, Damon spoke just loudly enough for everyone in the packed room to hear. "Actually, Mel-vin—" contempt dripped from his voice "—Ms. Birch isn't as impressed with my charm as you seem to be. She prefers my degree in structural engineering."

"Degree!" Mel snorted. "What kind of a degree do you have?"

"Mr. Free has a B.S. from Cal Tech," said a deep male voice. Thea recognized the man standing as the first person Damon had built a house for in Pine Butte. "With a minor in historic preservation and restoration."

"You expect me to believe—"

"Mel," Katey whispered urgently, her voice carrying easily to the front rows, "they wouldn't lie about something like that, something so easy to check."

"Cal Tech?" Bill said. "No fooling?"

"I'm professor emeritus there," the man continued. "Mr. Free was one of the best students I had in all my years of teaching."

"Well, okay," Mel said grudgingly. "So he studied something about restoring old buildings. But he's never done anything like that around here. He hasn't got any experience."

"You're mistaken in that, as well," said the professor. "Mr. Free took over a project for the city while he was a student of mine, saved a landmark building. He was presented with a commendation from the city of Pasadena." He made an expansive gesture around the room. "This town is fortunate to have someone with Mr. Free's talents willing to make his career here. He could earn far more money and prestige elsewhere."

Marsha stood up and began speaking hesitantly of Damon's character. Thea gave her a reassuring smile, but was too nervous to pay much attention to her words. She let her gaze sweep the room, and even in that quick glance, she saw that none of Damon's friends and customers would remain silent now. She looked at the reporters, busily scribbling in their notepads.

By tomorrow morning, everyone in Pine Butte would know what a fine man Damon Free had turned out to be, what fools they'd been not seeing what was right under their noses.

Thea heard the roar of Damon's motorcycle coming to life, the sound of gravel spraying as he sped from the parking lot. Her knees trembled and she had to sit down.

By tomorrow morning, Thea's heart would be broken. For she had broken Damon's trust. She hadn't just exposed him; she had forced him to expose himself to defend her. The sound of his motor faded into the distance, while she clamped her jaw to keep from crying. Thea had just destroyed the most beautiful thing that ever touched her life.

It wouldn't matter to Damon that she had done it for him. He'd made it very clear what tonight meant to him, practically begged her not to betray him. Pigheaded male though he was, his heart was fragile. No matter the reasons, she had knowingly inflicted on the man she loved the kind of wound that did not heal.

Somehow, Thea got through the interminable meeting. Her victory felt empty without Damon to share it. Marsha offered her a ride home, tactfully not mentioning why she needed one. As they left the building, Jerry approached her.

He shook her hand. "You did a good thing." He looked sad, and Thea noticed he didn't say Damon would get over it.

In Marsha's car, Thea sank into a gloom too deep for conversation. When she turned off the highway onto the gravel road, Marsha finally spoke.

"You're in love with him."

"Mmm."

"That's why you did this."

"Mmm."

Marsha stubbed her cigarette out in the overflowing ashtray. "Jerry's right, Thea. In the long run, it'll be good for

Damon that you forced the issue." She stopped her car in front of Thea's house.

"And for me?"

Marsha squeezed Thea's hand. "I wish I thought so."

"I wish I thought so, too."

As Thea stepped out of the car, Marsha said, "But you know he'll finish the house for you. Just the way he said."

Thea slumped into the wicker chair and watched Marsha's taillights disappear over the crest of the hill. She realized, with another twist of the knife she had stabbed through her own heart, that she had never doubted for a second that Damon would finish her restoration. He wouldn't back out of a job he had started.

Damon never went back on his word.

CHAPTER ELEVEN

GROANING, Thea pushed down the button on her alarm clock, wishing for those long summer days when 6:00 a.m. brought bright sunlight streaming into her room. Now this late in September, 6:00 a.m. was as dark as the middle of the night.

Thea rose, showering quickly and throwing on a pair of beat-up jeans and a paint-splattered gray sweatshirt. She tied her aggressively red hair into the ponytail that never held past ten o'clock.

For the past four months, Damon had arrived every morning at six-thirty on the dot. She always offered him coffee, which he never accepted. Then he'd politely tell her what she ought to get done that day. He'd warn her what workmen, if any, would be coming. He'd let her know what time he'd return that afternoon or evening and what he planned to get done.

The few mornings that Thea had overslept and failed to greet him, he'd left her a note with a list of chores. He never really left her too much to do, but she never had time to waste either. Some days—when she had other commitments, or when she simply burned out—she didn't finish.

Damon never burned out. He'd just complete her tasks before he started on the work he'd set himself, even if he had to stay till after midnight.

He always showed up exactly when he said he would, to the minute. He never let Thea help him with his work. He worked most weekends, saying he wouldn't finish otherwise, but he wouldn't let Thea do so. He *claimed* she

169

needed time off, but it was obvious he simply preferred to work alone.

He never complained, never swore, never raised his voice. He was so polite, Thea wanted to wring his neck. But he never gave her a chance, literally or figuratively. He was careful not to let their discussions last long enough for her to bring up anything personal.

Once or twice, Thea wondered if Damon held himself so fiercely aloof because he missed her, too, because he, too, longed for their former friendship and…intimacy. But the flashes of anger or hurt she saw on his face turned so quickly back to utter indifference, Thea knew better than to believe in what was surely just wishful thinking on her part.

As she watched her house gradually return to its former magnificence, Thea should have felt enormous satisfaction. Not just at being the owner of such a beautiful building, but at all she had contributed to it.

Certainly she felt awe. Damon treated her house as if it were a precious life, protecting each bit of its history from destruction or harm. Her house now would last another century, yet it looked just as it had the day it was finished the first time.

She had set the date for her grand opening, now two weeks away, sent invitations, announcements to the newspapers, to the travel agents she was working with back east. She had made herself a dress for the party, a formal, high-necked white Victorian gown with leg-of-mutton sleeves, hired a cateress, a band and a bartender. She had stayed up till the wee hours too many nights to count doing audits for her accounting firm to cover the cost of the party.

She had sat every night in Dora's window seat, telling herself she had done the right thing, assuring herself she should be proud of her success.

It hadn't helped. Peace was not hers. The past four

months had been the worst of Thea's life. Every day hurt worse than the last as she became more and more convinced Damon truly had cast her completely out of his heart.

This party should have been Damon's proudest moment. All of Pine Butte would come. No one in town would pass up this opportunity to see whether Damon was the hoodlum they remembered or the talented man they'd read about in the newspaper.

And everyone would see what an artist he truly was. Everyone—Thea had every confidence—would admire and praise his work. But *he* wouldn't even be there to hear it. Thea alone would listen to the astonished compliments, and most likely she would never even get a chance to pass them on to him. Stubborn, angry, mule-headed male that he was—hurt too, she had to admit—Damon would never allow her such an opportunity.

As bad as the past months had been, Thea knew the coming months, the coming years, would be even worse. For as horrible as it had been to see Damon day after day and have him treat her with such formal politeness, never once slipping and offering her a moment of tenderness or even friendship, never ever touching her...at least he'd been here. In a few weeks when the work was finished, she would never see him again.

Flopping on her bed, Thea closed her eyes, determined not to cry. She hated it when she had to greet Damon in the morning with red eyes. He'd asked her once politely— oh so politely—if she had allergies.

With only two hours' sleep the night before, Thea had been too tired to keep her mouth shut. "Yes, Damon," she'd snapped, "I'm allergic to stubborn male idiots who don't know what's good for them."

Damon had nodded sympathetically. "Best to stay away from them, then." He immediately changed the subject back to plaster versus drywall.

Suddenly, Thea sat up and glared at the clock. It was after seven! She must have fallen back to sleep. She leapt out of bed and ran downstairs.

Damon had obviously been there. He'd started the coffeemaker and brewed her a fresh pot, but he hadn't taken a cup for himself. His work gloves were on the kitchen table, but he hadn't left her a note with a list of chores.

He must think she didn't need a note today, Thea realized, pouring herself a cup of coffee that she hoped would make her brain work. She'd been painting since Tuesday, and so had Damon—she doing the lower floors, he the upper.

Gulping caffeine, she went outside, squinting at the sun just coming over the top of Mount Anthony. Every morning, Damon left a clean paintbrush, a gallon of paint, a paint tray and two or three pairs of rubber gloves next to the short ladder she used. He even positioned the ladder for her at the spot where she'd left off the day before.

Today as she circled her house, she found none of that. The only ladder was the long extension ladder he used for the second floor. But today, he'd extended it to the attic, to the canvas siding just beneath the highest eave.

Thea gulped at the sight of it.

She walked all the way around the house again. She doubted she could have missed something as large as her ladder, but perhaps he'd left the paint can where it wasn't obvious. Feeling like an idiot, she even looked behind the shrubs near the siding she'd been painting yesterday.

She found nothing. Damon obviously expected her to paint the canvas today, so he could nail the stabilizing boards across it tonight. No doubt he'd left everything here so she would get it done first thing and the paint would be dry when he arrived.

She stared up to the top of the ladder, which looked terrifyingly far away from where she stood, and saw that the paint and brush and gloves were already up there, hanging from a top bar. Her head spun. She attributed it to drinking coffee so fast on an empty stomach.

But she couldn't eat anything now, not the way she felt about that ladder. She had to get this done. She would not let Damon do her work for her again.

Putting her coffee mug down at the foot of the ladder, Thea began to climb. Really, she assured herself, it wasn't that different from climbing the short ladder. Three times. Maybe four. Perhaps she should count steps, then she'd know for sure. She could pat herself on the back later for climbing so high.

She took another step—surely her two thousandth—and the ladder swayed inward. Thea didn't shriek, but only because her voice stuck. She certainly tried to shriek. She tried to move. She tried to open her eyes.

The only thing she could make her body do was grip the ladder tighter. Her hands hurt from clutching the metal, but she assured herself that was good. At least she hadn't fainted.

"Thea?" Damon's voice, not quite as polite as usual, floated up to her.

She tried to answer. Her mouth opened and shut.

"Thea!" He actually sounded worried. Didn't he? Was it just her imagination?

"D-aaaa..." Thea squeaked.

"Goddammit, woman, what the hell are you doing up there on that ladder?"

It wasn't her imagination. He sounded furious. Not cold, not polite, not reserved. Furious. Intensely involved in the situation.

He sounded like Damon.

Relief flooded Thea, mixing with her terror. She began to tremble all over. Her right foot slipped and she screamed.

Leaning forward, she wrapped her arms tightly around the ladder but—sensibly—kept her eyes closed.

"Come down here this minute!"

Emotions swirled through Thea with the power of a tidal wave—fear uppermost perhaps, but joy close behind. Relief, happiness, dread that Damon's coldness would return the moment she set foot on solid ground. Even through all that, Thea recognized what a stupid thing Damon had just said.

For some reason, that helped her find her voice. "Damon, of all the foolish things you've said in your life, that is the dumbest."

"You're probably right." He swore under his breath. She could tell, though she couldn't hear the oaths. "Don't move."

Thea would laugh about this if she ever got down, she knew she would. "I didn't think you could say anything dumber, but you just did."

"I'll be right there." He began to climb.

His weight bowed the ladder forward, and Thea clamped her jaw shut to keep from crying out at the sensation.

"It's okay, Thea," Damon called up to her, his voice gentle now, reassuring. "The ladder can hold six or seven of us. You're totally safe."

"You're such a liar, Damon," Thea managed in spite of the fear roiling in her stomach with every sway of the ladder.

"We-ell, maybe not *totally* safe," Damon said as if he was thinking it over. "Because when I get you down on the ground, I am going to turn you over my knee."

"Ha-ha, very funny," Thea said weakly.

"You think I'm joking?" Damon said, his voice coming closer with each word. "Actually, you're in more danger of that than you are of falling off this ladder."

"Oh, good," Thea said. "I'll worry about that instead

of the way the ladder bobs around when you— Oooooh, Damon.''

His strong, wonderful, secure arms slid around her, holding her tightly between him and the ladder. "God, Thea," he breathed in her ear, "are you all right?"

"I am now." She wanted to let go of the ladder, turn all the way around and hug Damon with all her strength. Of course, she couldn't. So she simply turned her head into the crook of his throat and kissed him over and over. "This is the most all right I've been for months."

"Yeah?" Damon said, doing nothing to push her away. "Well, it's not going to last."

"Oh, Damon," Thea whimpered, pressing against him as hard as she could. "Please don't tell me you're turning back into that iceman as soon as we're on the ground. Damon, please."

"I can't," he said, his tone long-suffering but resigned. "I'm not strong enough. I've fought it as hard as I can. But I don't have the strength to let you go again. But you must know we've got one helluva big fight ahead of us."

"Fight," Thea murmured, nuzzling his throat again. "Mmm, okay, I can handle that."

"You think."

"Mmm."

"Dammit, Thea, stop kissing me," Damon said, his voice sharp with exasperation, "and start trying to get off this ladder. Move your right foot down a step. I'll hold you."

"You'll hold me all the way down?"

"Of course I will." Damon's voice shifted back and forth from exasperated to husky as Thea continued nibbling along his whiskery throat.

"And on the ground?"

"I think you can hold yourself up on the ground, don't you?"

"That's not much incentive, Damon," Thea said, letting her pout show in her voice. "You'll hold me on the ladder and you'll let me go on the ground? I've spent four months wanting so bad for you to hold me it hurt to be around you, and now you think I'll just walk down this ladder so you can let me go again?" She tightened her grip on the ladder.

Beneath her cheek, Damon's jaw clenched, relaxed, clenched. "I really *should* turn you over my knee."

"Up here?"

"Prebble, *please* don't make me carry you down this damn contraption."

Prebble. He called her Prebble. Her heart fluttered, making her voice come out breathy. "Do you promise to hold me on the ground...as long as I want to be held?"

He chuckled. Thea felt it, she heard it, she shivered with pleasure at the sensation. Damon's chuckle—it had been so long since she'd heard it.

"Yes, dammit, I'll hold you as long as you want." The chuckle left Damon's voice. "Then I swear I will describe to you, in the most infinitesimal detail, at the top of my voice, exactly why I am still furious with you."

Thea winced. "Then will you hold me some more?"

"After that," Damon said grimly, "I'm not sure you'll want me to."

CHAPTER TWELVE

WHEN both her feet hit blessed earth, Thea spun into Damon's arms, clinging to him with love and relief and the fear that he might let her go. And she'd die if he did that, she knew she would.

If she didn't die from holding him. After four months of denial, desire replaced relief with a speed that stunned her. In seconds, Thea found herself weak-kneed from want.

Damon responded with restraint.

Oh, his *body* reacted the way a man's body did, and pressed against the length of him the way she was, Thea couldn't help knowing that. But she also knew he held her with only his arms. Inside, where it mattered, he held her not at all.

She wanted to cry. But she didn't let go. It might be the last time she ever got to hold Damon.

"Why in the name of God did you climb up there?" he snapped, his irritation definitely not extinguished.

"I couldn't find my ladder...you didn't leave me a note." Thea kept her face buried in his chest. "I thought you wanted me to paint."

"You thought *what*?" He sounded a lot more than irritated now. "You thought I would ask you to do something that *terrified* you?" He grabbed her shoulders and held her where he could glare at her. "What the hell made you decide I'd turned into a torturer?"

"My paint stuff wasn't anywhere," Thea said. "And you've already done so much of my work. I didn't want you to have to do more because I...wimped out."

His hands tightened on her shoulders, making her wince. He swore and let her go.

"You finished the ground floor, Thea," he said. "The upper stories aren't your work, they're mine. I agreed to do it. I gave my word."

"Oh, Damon," Thea exclaimed, "stop saying that!"

"And you don't wimp out," he continued as if she hadn't said a word, "when you let a phobia affect your actions. You wimp out when you let other people push you around."

"Push me around?" Four months of silence made Thea's voice louder than she would have wished. Now that they were talking, she couldn't bear to waste time talking about paint. "Who? The city council? They didn't push me, Damon. You did."

"Yeah, right," he said. "You couldn't handle the stress of taking a position by yourself. Standing on your own, out of the crowd. Having to fight for what's rightfully yours. Wanted everything tied up nice and clean, follow the rules, make sure everyone in authority is happy." He cursed and turned his back. "If you betray a few friends along the way, you can always get more, right? Nice conventional ones who won't embarrass you."

"Damon Free, that's not even close to the truth. I didn't do it for me. I did it for you." She pounded on his back. "Turn around and talk to me, you big coward."

He shook his head, then strode toward the gazebo under the big cottonwood tree. Unlike most of his work on the house, the gazebo was a reproduction. The original had been too rotted to save.

Thea watched him go, seeing pain in the stiffness of his movements. She heard it, too, in his voice; saw it in his eyes when he spoke of betrayal.

For months, Thea had prayed that Damon's feelings for her, whatever they were, had survived the city council meeting. But as the days kept passing, she had become convinced that no remnant of his feelings remained.

Now, stabs of hope made her almost too scared to follow him. But she had to find out. Oh, please, God, he wouldn't act so hurt if he didn't care, would he?

She followed him to the gazebo and sat next to him. He moved and sat across from her. Stubbornly, she reached across the space and put a hand on his knee.

"I thought you didn't want to let me go," she said.

"Oh, I *want* to, Thea," he said. His jaw clenched so tight, a muscle jumped in his cheek. "I'm not sure I can." He raised his dark, wounded gaze to her. "That's where I am, babe. I can't let you go, I can't let you in—not all the way inside where it counts. How can I trust you? Ever again?"

Tears burned Thea's eyes. She blinked rapidly, not letting them fall. Damon leaned forward, taking her hands in both of his.

"Answer me, please," he said. "If you've got an answer. How can I trust you?"

His grip on her fingers hurt, but she doubted he knew it. He hurt more in a worse place: his heart. And no matter how well her actions that night had turned out, Damon couldn't forget that she had completely disregarded his feelings.

"Damon." She tugged a hand free to put on his cheek. "I almost held my tongue. I knew you wanted me to slink out of there with you, still hiding. But when I looked at you, that's not what I saw."

"You didn't look hard enough."

"I saw pain. Damon, it radiated off you. And I knew that from the outside, where you'd locked yourself, you'd never know how unnecessary all that pain was." She sniffed back her tears. "I couldn't let you go on suffering. No matter what it did to me, I couldn't."

"To you? You got exactly what you wanted," he said, the anger in his voice changing to disappointment.

"Exactly what I wanted?" Thea cried. "You know that's not true. I lost—"

"What about me?" he interrupted, jabbing his chest. "How much do you think I lost? At least you made the choice for yourself."

Thea deflated. "That's true, Damon." She swallowed. "But I knew in the long run it would make you happier. Well, at least satisfied and comfortable."

She closed her eyes a moment, visualizing Damon as he had looked that night: unbelievably handsome, of course, but hostile. The memory made her stomach twist. If even half that hostility remained, how could she ever make him believe she'd had his best interests at heart?

"Happy?" Damon pulled away from her and stood, leaning over her. "God, Thea. Don't you listen to anything? In that whole room, the only thing I wanted was you. And you betrayed me. All that—" he gestured in a frustrated way toward Pine Butte "—respectability. It doesn't mean anything without you."

Thea's heart stuttered, missing beats. Then it raced as if trying to catch up. She didn't think her knees would work, but she stood up, wanting to get closer to him.

"Mmeeee?" It came out a squeak. "Me?"

"Of course you!" He grabbed her fiercely, angrily, by the upper arms. "What do you think this is all about? Why do you think I give a damn?"

"Oh, Damon," Thea said, trying to eliminate the space between them despite his grip on her arms. "I...how should I have known?"

"How could you miss it?"

"I missed it, you obstinate male, because you never said a word!"

"You had to know," Damon said dismissively, but with, at last, a scrap of hesitation in his voice. "Didn't you?"

He relaxed his guard a second, and Thea squirmed between his arms and onto his chest. "You know what I thought when I looked at you that night?" she asked. "I thought, he's so kind, and he's so incredibly beautiful, and he's—" she felt heat rushing into her cheeks "—the sexiest thing in the northwest. He can have a hundred women. But this is the only chance he'll ever have to prove himself to his hometown."

Damon's hand cupped the back of her head and tilted her eyes up to his. "Don't you get it, Thea? I don't want a hundred women. I want you."

Thea stared into the dark charcoal irises she hadn't seen this close in way too long. "I love you so much, Damon, I couldn't let you go on hurting yourself. Even if I lost any chance of ever making you love me back, I couldn't be that selfish. I wouldn't ever forgive myself." Tears filled her eyes again, but she refused to shed them. "You knew how I felt, Damon. How could you possibly believe I acted only out of selfishness?"

"You knew how I felt, too, Thea," Damon said. "How could I believe anything else?"

Thea shook her head. "Even during all these horrible days when you wouldn't let me tell you I loved you, I still knew I'd done the right thing for you. Even if it took you fifty years to admit it."

"Fifty years," Damon exploded. "That's the point. What were you going to do during those fifty years? Wait?" He made a disgusted noise of disbelief. "Or find someone else to rub my nose in what we could have had, slap me daily with the knowledge of how much you threw away that night?"

"Someone else?" Thea laughed. It came out breathy and shaky, but it conveyed just as much disbelief as Damon's snort. "Like my mother? Going frantically from man to man, looking for the consummate love. Not a chance. Auntie taught me that lesson only too well. When you find perfection in love, you don't ever look for it again."

Damon stared at her, suspicion slowly fading from his expression. "Are you trying to make me believe you'd have spent your life alone?"

"Of course I would, Damon," Thea said. "It'd be easier to live my life alone than to try to find another man I'd love as much as I love you. I wouldn't waste my time."

The side of his lips twitched into that lazy half grin she hadn't seen since early summer. The sight made Thea's fingertips tingle with the desire to trace the outline of his beautiful mouth.

"Give me this again, Prebble," Damon said, trying to sound nonchalant and only partly succeeding. "Start with how much you love me and work up to how you'll pine away forever if you can't have me."

Tell him again? Thea's voice tightened till she could hardly get it out. "Damon, you idiot, I've wanted to tell you for months. You wouldn't let me."

His arms surrounded her, holding her tenderly but fiercely. She ached to believe he would never let her go again. "C'mon, Prebble," he whispered. "Tell me again."

"If you want, I'll tell you every other minute until you get tired of hearing it. Damon, I love you. I love you so much I can't think of anything else most of the time."

"So that's it," Damon said, nodding as if he'd just figured something out.

"That's what?"

He chuckled. "That's why I had to redo half the wallpaper you put up."

"You didn't," she protested.

"Every night after you fell asleep." He rolled his eyes. "About two-thirds probably."

"Damon Free, you did not."

He sat down on the bench and pulled her into his lap. "You'll never know, will you?"

Before she could answer, his lips covered hers. The kiss she had dreamed every night for months faded instantly from her mind as the real-life one consumed her. Damon's hands moved over her body, pulling her closer, touching her hips, her waist, the sides of her breasts. One palm moved to the back of her head while the other stayed low and tight on her spine. Damon held her as securely as if she was trying to get away.

But she didn't try. She wanted nothing more than to remain forever in Damon's arms, never to let him take his lips from hers, to indulge eternally these swirling wants shooting through her.

At last, Damon pulled gently away. "Prebble?"

"Mmm," Thea moaned, praying Damon wasn't going to suggest they go all the way upstairs to her bed before he made love to her. "It's private here."

"Actually, sweet," he whispered into her hair, "the kid I hired to paint the gables is standing over by the ladder waiting for me."

"Kid?" Thea blinked. "Kid!" She sat up straight, pushing her wild hair more or less into place. "Damon, you knew all along he was there, didn't you?"

He took her chin and kissed her lips. "Don't wimp out on me now, Prebble. Why don't you go wait for me upstairs? I won't be long." He put her on her feet.

"No." Thea put a hand on his shoulder while she regained her equilibrium. "I'm going to call Father."

"Father?" Damon choked. "And tell him what? What we're about to do?"

Thea giggled. "Not in so many words." She stroked his cheek. "Trust me."

Inside, she decided to use the phone in the front parlor.

With Damon's artistry, it had become the most beautiful room Thea had ever seen.

The walnut wainscoting gleamed. The ornate crown molding Damon had preserved or perfectly matched, she'd painted a delicate ivory. For the walls—plastered not dry-walled—she'd chosen a lovely deep blue-green. She had painstakingly reupholstered the antique Chinese love seat with some material she and Dora had bought in San Francisco three years ago. Damon had removed the paint from the stones in the fireplace with enough care to save the lichens underneath.

Thea loved this room. In here, she felt Damon had truly brought her and Auntie's dream to life. What better place to tell Father she had found the man of her dreams?

"Father?" she said when Norman answered. "I have something to tell you."

"Prebble?" Damon said, entering the room. He quieted when he saw she was on the phone.

"Who's that, Theadora?" Norman asked. "It's not eight hundred hours there, is it? That's early for a man to be visiting. Has he been there all night? I hope you haven't called to tell me you've gotten yourself in trouble."

Thea's jaw hung open. She couldn't believe Father's re-action. How dare he try to destroy the most beautiful morning of her life? "Really, Father! I am long past the age of consent."

"That may be true," Norman said. "But you are the sole representative of the family in Pine Butte now, and we expect you to live up to the high standards—"

"I've heard all I need to about family standards!" Thea interrupted. "In fact, I'd heard enough by the time I was thirteen to have memorized the speech." She took a breath. "Goodbye, Father. You have insulted my intelligence for the last time. Call me back when you respect me."

She slammed down the phone. When Damon came toward her, she walked away, too angry even to let him comfort her.

"Hey, Prebble," Damon said softly from behind her, "don't you think I know how you feel? I spent most of my life feeling exactly the way you do now."

Thea spun and looked him directly in the eye. "Do you still, Damon?"

"Uh…no." Damon actually looked sheepish. "You were right about that. This middle-class stuff *is*…comfortable. It kind of grows on you."

She narrowed her eyes. "You mean it's true?"

"What's true?"

"I heard you hired on as one of the extra deputies over the Labor Day Fair."

"That's nothing." He grabbed her hand and pulled her toward him. "The real shocker is Mel and I are on speaking terms. Matt's dad came to the meeting. He told Mel—"

"The truth?" Thea said, stunned.

"He didn't go that far," Damon said. "But he told him to let go of the hate. Matt's even spent a couple of nights at my place." He ran a hand over her disheveled hair. "The guys, too, their wives especially. They really enjoy being respectable. I'd have done this a long time ago if I knew it hurt them. I never expected anyone else to fight my battles for me."

"They're all very loyal to you, Damon. They didn't mind."

"That's what they say, too, but they like it better now." He tugged gently on the useless rubber band, freeing her hair from the remains of the ponytail. "Want me to call your old man?"

Thea shook her head. "I'll do it."

As she punched the numbers into the phone again, she swore this time to stay on the subject.

"Colonel Birch," her father answered.

"I didn't get to tell you, Father. The man you heard is Damon Free, the boy you threw out of Dora's house years ago. I love him very, very much. Since you asked, though it's none of your business, he hasn't actually spent the night. But only because he hasn't asked. When he does, I will definitely answer yes."

Not wanting her father to spoil such a declaration, Thea hung up. Just in time to feel Damon's arms come around her from behind, his lips caressing her neck beneath her hair.

"Nicely done, Prebble," he said, laughing through his kisses. "Really opened the lines of communication. All that give-and-take. Couldn't have done it better myself."

"Oh, Damon," Thea said, turning in his arms, "shut up and kiss me."

Damon obliged.

The phone rang. With their lips still joined, Damon picked up the receiver and held it where they both could hear.

"Mmm?" Thea managed.

"I ought to tell you something, too, Theadora," Norman said, making Thea tense. "I should have made this clear years ago. I suppose I thought I had. I love you very much, also, and I'm proud of you. If Damon is the man you love, I'm sure he's right for you. If he doesn't love you as much as you love him, just let me know, and I'll have a Ranger division there at dawn."

Thea opened her mouth to speak, but the only sound she could force out was, "Oh."

"Thank you, sir," Damon answered for her. "That's the nicest wedding present you could give her...us."

When he hung up, Thea stared at him, trying to marshal her thoughts. "Damon—what did you say? Have you ever said that...ever before?"

Damon's smile spread slowly from his lips to his eyes.

"Said what, Prebble? Wedding? Of course I've never said it before." He took her face gently between his palms. "Why would I? I'll never say it again, either. One wedding this lifetime will do for me."

Thea shook her head. "Not that word, Damon. The other…'Sir'. Have you ever said that before?"

He rolled his eyes. "Not that I remember." He shrugged, and this time it actually looked relaxed. "But that was a hard phone call for him to make—he must have known I'd be listening."

Thea hugged Damon till he grunted. "Oh, thank you, Damon. That's the nicest wedding present you could give me. That is, unless you want to…I mean, you wouldn't consider, er, calling your own father, would you?"

Damon's voice turned cold. "Don't press your luck, Prebble. Life isn't a fairy tale."

He slipped an arm around her waist and began leading her toward the stairs. At the foot, he turned her toward him. The distrust she saw in his eyes made Thea want to kick herself for ever mentioning his father.

He slid his fingers through her hair, leaving his hand at the back of her neck. "I think this taught us a lot about how to love each other. Four months licking my wounds is probably a bit too long. Agreed?"

"Of course it is, Damon. Four minutes is all I'll give you next time."

He nodded. "That's what I wonder about—next time." His eyes turned so serious they seemed to bore holes into hers. "There won't really be a next time, will there? Not like this—your going back on your word?"

"I didn't go back on my word, Damon," Thea insisted. "I wouldn't. But if you mean next time I see you behaving in a way that I know hurts you just because you're being a stubborn, pigheaded male, will I just sit there with my mouth shut?"

Damon's brows lowered, but the resulting glare did not frighten Thea an iota. "I wouldn't phrase it exactly that way."

"I doubt you would," Thea said. "But I guess you know the answer. Of *course* I'll never let you suffer that way, not if there's anything I can do about it. If I had to go to that meeting again, I'd do the same thing all over again."

Damon's frown darkened briefly, then melted altogether. He threw back his head and laughed. Then he reached behind her knees and lifted her into his chest.

As he started up the stairs with her in his arms, he muttered ferociously about what he really ought to do to Thea, but she didn't mind. She didn't think that's what he had any intention of doing.

In her room, Damon proved her right. When he lowered her to the bed and covered her melting body with his hard male one, Thea had no hesitation at all. Many of the decisions she'd made since she met Damon had been difficult—this one was easy.

Though Thea came new to this kind of love, love with the body as well as the heart, Damon answered all her questions...before she asked them. He answered with his lips and his tongue and his hands. The most intimate questions, he answered with incredible tenderness with the most masculine parts of his body.

And Thea's body responded willingly, joyfully, taking all of him, giving him all she could of herself, of her soul. When she thought she could take no more, Damon spun them together through a swirl of pleasure to someplace perfect. No thoughts penetrated those spiraling waves of sensation too delirious to define.

But later, when she drifted through a softness of slowly decreasing ripples, one thought formed in her mind, one thought she managed to murmur from lips she wasn't sure would work.

"Only you, Damon. I told you I'd found perfection."

Still atop her, he raised himself on his elbows, kissing her eyelids. "Damn right, only me. Don't ever forget it, Prebble." He kissed her deeply. "And that wasn't perfection, just the best it's ever been in my life. We'll have to practice constantly to achieve perfection."

Thea opened her eyes to gaze at him. "Do you always joke at serious times? Or are you just afraid to say it? You haven't yet, you know."

Damon's eyes took on a suspicious sheen. "I love you? Is that what you haven't heard me say? God, Thea, I love you so much I don't know how to say it. I didn't know there was this much love in the world, much less that I could fit it all in one heart. I'll never stop loving you. I'll never stop wondering how I got so lucky. I may not deserve you, but don't get the idea that means I'll ever let you get away."

Thea didn't fight her tears this time. "We'll have to keep practicing this part, too, Damon."

He smiled. "If you want, love, I'll say it three times a day for the rest of your life."

"Only three times?" Thea pouted.

"Do you always joke at serious moments?" Damon chuckled.

Pulling her to him, he began another lesson in how to say "I love you" without words.

Take 4 bestselling love stories FREE

Plus get a FREE surprise gift!

HARLEQUIN WOMEN KNOW ROMANCE WHEN THEY SEE IT.

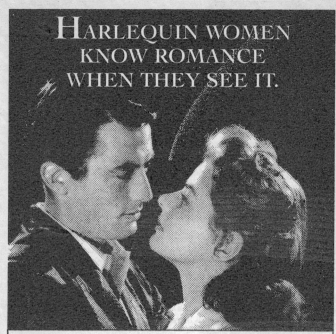

And they'll see it on **ROMANCE CLASSICS**, the new 24-hour TV channel devoted to romantic movies and original programs like the special **Romantically Speaking-Harlequin® Goes Prime Time.**

Romantically Speaking-Harlequin® Goes Prime Time introduces you to many of your favorite romance authors in a program developed exclusively for Harlequin® readers.

Watch for **Romantically Speaking-Harlequin® Goes Prime Time** beginning in the summer of 1997.

If you're not receiving ROMANCE CLASSICS, call your local cable operator or satellite provider and ask for it today!

Escape to the network of your dreams.

As Seen on TV!

Free Gift Offer

With a Free Gift proof-of-purchase from any Harlequin® book, you can receive a beautiful cubic zirconia pendant.

This stunning marquise-shaped stone is a genuine cubic zirconia—accented by an 18" gold tone necklace.
(Approximate retail value $19.95)

Send for yours today...
compliments of ◆HARLEQUIN®

To receive your free gift, a cubic zirconia pendant, send us one original proof-of-purchase, photocopies not accepted, from the back of any Harlequin Romance®, Harlequin Presents®, Harlequin Temptation®, Harlequin Superromance®, Harlequin Intrigue®, Harlequin American Romance®, or Harlequin Historicals® title available at your favorite retail outlet, together with the Free Gift Certificate, plus a check or money order for $1.65 U.S./$2.15 CAN. (do not send cash) to cover postage and handling, payable to Harlequin Free Gift Offer. We will send you the specified gift. Allow 6 to 8 weeks for delivery. Offer good until December 31, 1997, or while quantities last. Offer valid in the U.S. and Canada only.

Free Gift Certificate

Name: _____

Address: _____

City: _____ State/Province: _____ Zip/Postal Code: _____

Mail this certificate, one proof-of-purchase and a check or money order for postage and handling to: HARLEQUIN FREE GIFT OFFER 1997. In the U.S.: 3010 Walden Avenue, P.O. Box 9071, Buffalo NY 14269-9057. In Canada: P.O. Box 604, Fort Erie, Ontario L2Z 5X3.

FREE GIFT OFFER   084-KEZ

ONE PROOF-OF-PURCHASE

To collect your fabulous FREE GIFT, a cubic zirconia pendant, you must include this original proof-of-purchase for each gift with the properly completed Free Gift Certificate.

084-KEZR